THE ALEUT

by

JENABE E. CALDWELL

Other publications by the author
From Night to Knight
Follow the Instructions
The Story of The Báb and Bahá'u'lláh

THE ALEUT

A Historical Novel of the Aleut People
By
Jenabe E. Caldwell

BEST PUBLISHER
3-2-7 Yamamoto
Utsunomiya, Japan

ISBN 0-9762780-0-6

First Edition

TABLE OF CONTENTS THE ALEUT

FORWARD

The following historical story tells of the tragic persecution and eventual genocide of the Aleut people in the Aleutian Islands.

Thousands of Aleuts were killed in the genocide including little boys over the age of six. Many also died from contagious diseases such as pneumonia, smallpox, cholera and venereal disease brought in through first contact with the Russians. Even the common cold was introduced through this contact. Smallpox alone wiped out entire villages.

My home was in the Aleutians for twenty seven years from 1953. I learned firsthand of the suffering, the persecution and the genocide from the older Aleuts. This story is based on historical fact.

The "Holy Tree" that the Aleuts worshiped at on Umnak Island was a real tree. When I was there, the little house with no windows or doors was still standing in the churchyard in Nikolski and through the cracks one could see the remains of a tree stump.

The way Unalaska got its name dates back to when the Russians came. Not knowing where they had landed and they asked the Aleuts what was this place and were told it is Oonalaska, in the Aleut language this means little land. Then when they pointed to the east and asked what was over there, the answer was Alaska, which in the Aleut language means great land. Of course anyone who has lived in Alaska and then comes out to Unalaska will say that this is the most Unalaska place they have ever seen.

That Umnak was the Island of peace is a historical fact. The migration of the people to Umnak from the far west, from the far east and from the Pribilofs in the north was a real factor in keeping the Aleut race healthy as it prevented too much inter-marriage and kept them in contact with a common language. Umnak was like Israel is for some religions such as Jews, Christians, Moslems and Bahá'ís.

This story had its beginning before the Russians arrived in the Aleutians.

Kung stood among the damp trees in the deep forest on his island home of Kodiak. He put his arms around one of the trees and meditated about Agoo-Gook. What was this creator of all that is? Why? What for? Why had the Great Teacher of the distant past told the Aleuts about the connection of Himself with that one lone Tree that grew on the Island of Umnak? Why that particular Tree? What made that Tree special? Why wasn't this Tree that he now embraced the same? The great Agoo-Gook, through His Teacher, instructed the people that once during their lifetime all must visit that Tree. He further taught the people that the Island of Umnak was His Holy Land and, therefore, it was forbidden to fight or kill there.

Tomorrow Kung's family, his mother, father, little sister and he would embark on the great adventure to Umnak. Many people had gone before, but some never returned, having been lost in the tides, perished in bad weather while traversing the vast distances between Kodiak and Umnak.

This journey would take him and his family over 1450 kilometers over some of the most ferocious seas known to man. The cold and freezing air rushes down from the Arctic across the Bering Sea, which is met at the Aleutian Chain by the hot air currents which rushes up from the warm Pacific Ocean, creating winds of typhoon velocities. These hurricane force winds are often accompanied by freezing rain, snow and sleet, are further intensified by the tide waters moving in and out of the narrow Aleutian passes. The active volcanoes and earthquakes add to the tremendous hazards that Kung and his family would encounter on this perilous journey.

His questions unanswered, Kung reluctantly let go of his hold on the tree, picked up his spear and moved off silently into the mist-shrouded drizzle of rain.

Suddenly, all or his faculties were sharpened at the distinct sound of something coming through the forest toward him. Kung brought up his spear and ready for instant action he froze as immobile and silent as the trees around him. Through the drizzle of rain came one of the small Kodiak deer and it came directly towards Kung. When this small animal was within 20 feet, Kung let go with his spear, and the animal was his. Surely this was a good omen and a special gift from the great Agoo-Gook. Although Kung was only 17 years old he was considered a man, just that spring he had gone through the sweat lodge ceremony that marked his manhood. He was now considered a major provider for the people.

Kung easily picked up the small deer, threw it over his shoulder and returned to his barabara. He carefully hung his deer in a tree and several women, including his mother, came out and started the task of butchering it. Kung was very happy that he had such good fortune for now, when they started their longed-for Pilgrimage to Umnak, they could go with some fresh meat.

He entered into the barabara by backing down the five steps. One never entered a barabara going down front-wards. One always entered with his back exposed to show his faith and trust of the people in the barabara. Although it was built underground, the place was warm and cozy. It had the familiar smells of home, the warm smell of wood burning, the body odors of his loved ones, the smell of the seal oil, and the smell of fish and venison that hung from the ceiling drying and smoking.

Kung quickly removed all his clothes as was the custom and washed himself. As his eyes adjusted to the gloom and the light coming in from the doorway and from the fire and seal oil lamps that provided not only heat but light, he saw his father busily packing. He was cleaning and securing his spears, knives and fishing gear. The badarky, a boat, they would be using was large as badarkies went. In fact, this one was made of whale bone and seal hides by Kung and his father and it had holes for two rowers. Most of these badarkies had only one hole and were made for just one person to row and to carry. However, their badarky, would require both men to carry it even when it was empty.

His father greeted his son with the customary,

"Ang, and what have you been doing?"

Kung replied, "I went into the trees and wondered about Agoo-Gook and why this one Tree in Umnak is different from all the other trees here on Kodiak. I thought about the start of our Pilgrimage tomorrow and that Agoo-Gook sent me a deer as a sign."

Kung's father was pleased with this son of his and he smiled deep within himself, but no expression showed on his lined and weather-beaten face. His only response was a grunt.

Kung started to help his father with the work, and the feeling that both men experienced was a content companionship. Dinner was served and even his little ten year old sister was busy. Darkness descended and the drizzle turned into a soft patter of rain. The conversation centered around the greatest event in their lives--the longed for and anticipated Pilgrimage to the great and Holy Tree of Umnak. Finally, Kung dropped off to sleep and dreamed about trees, animals and badarkies all mixed up with a beautiful woman.

The twilight just before dawn found Kung and his family up. The two-man badarky was already launched, the provisions were wrapped in water-tight seal gut sacks and placed in the badarky, along with their knives, spears and tools for making new instruments as they would be needed. The sun slowly rose into one of those rare and beautiful spring days with out a cloud in the sky. The other members of the village slowly gathered on the beach. Some brought good luck charms and some who had made the Pilgrimage before, offered their last bits of advice.

First, Kung's mother went into the badarky through one of the holes in the bow, followed by his sister. Then Kung entered the first hole, and from his waist up he was out of the badarky. Then his father pushed the badarky out into the sea and went into the last hole.

After waving goodbye to their friends and relatives, Kung and his father began to paddle with strong firm strokes that sent the badarky skimming across the sea. The blue sky, the cry of the sea gulls, the shimmering ocean and the sun-warmed breeze fanning his face caused shivers to run up and down Kung's spine. This feeling was intensified by the knowledge that they were embarking on the Holy Quest to Agoo-Gook's Holy Tree.

As they traveled north northwest, they had no compass and no navigation charts of any kind, yet they held their course by a natural instinct born only to true children of the sea. The day's progress was sure and steady, and from time to time they encountered big herds of sea lion. Several times during the day they even saw some whales. When they became hungry, Kung's mother would pass some dried fish, smoked venison or jerky up from the bottom of the boat. All day Kung and his father both rowed. Occasionally, one would stop for a brief rest and the other one would row.

As night descended and the cool of night began to touch their bodies they fit themselves into water proof shirts made of seal gut that were actually part of the badarky. They tied themselves into them so that the only exposed part of their bodies were their faces. These shirts even had hoods that covered most of their faces when needed. In fact, when they were inside these shirts, they became part of the badarky.

When Kung became exhausted, he signaled his father accordingly and slipped down into the bottom of the badarky, tied up the shirt over the hatch and was instantly in a deep and dreamless sleep.

After a while, Kung's little sister shook him and told him that he must relieve daddy. Kung was up instantly. After drinking some water and eating a little, he slipped back into his seal-gut shirt, signaled his father, and as the father slipped into the bottom of the badarky to sleep, Kung took up the lonely vigil of long, hard rowing.

Each day came on clear and sunny with a gentle breeze out of the southeast that helped move them along. They always kept a baited line in the water for occasionally they were able to catch fresh fish to supplement the dried and smoked food they had on board. Sometimes they would capture sea birds, ducks and geese so they would also have fresh meat. They lived off of the sea on a day-to-day basis also eating kelp and sea-weed.

As the weather held steady, sometimes Kung's mother and sister would take their turns at rowing. This gave them exercise and got them out of the bottom of the boat into the fresh air and sunshine. The Pilgrims for the first four days made good time averaging 30 to 40 kilometers a day.

On the fifth day the sky began to cloud up, and the wind shifted from the north so the tiny two man badarky turned into the wind that was now picking up in velocity. It also began to rain. The rain was welcome as they were able to fill all their water bags with fresh water. By noon the waves, sea and wind were driving the tiny craft to the south. Kung got out of his shirt and using the hand holds, he went forward on his stomach and put out the sea anchor. This sea anchor was like a large seal-skin bag which trailed off the front of the badarky and sank below the surface, filling with water and producing a drag to slow the drift to the south, and kept the bow into the wind to prevent the waves from hitting them broadside. The two men, as the magnitude of the storm increased, watched the waves, and as they attacked their badarky, skillfully navigated the sea wave by wave.

At one time an exceptionally big wave turned them broadside. Before they were able to straighten out the badarky the next wave caught them, lifted them into the air and turned the craft upside down. The sea anchor caught and put the bow back into the wind, and the two men in skilled unison, using their paddles righted the boat. Only a small amount of water got inside of the tight little craft, and the seal skin shirts kept them dry. These men were justifiably proud of the skill with which they had fashioned their badarky for this trip.

By midnight the storm began to die down, and although the wind still blew out of the north it was losing its strength. So both men tied up their seal skin hatches and retired exhausted to the bottom of the badarky and fell into an exhausted sleep. The sea anchor held the badarky into the wind while the family slept.

The morning dawned overcast with a cold rain and a steady wind still out of the north. When the men awoke they took up the toil of trying to regain as much distance as they could. Kung reversed the process of putting out the sea anchor and took it in while his father held the badarky into the wind and waves. The wind was not strong but by rowing hard and steadily throughout the next three days they did little more than just hold their own. They traveled maybe about 4 or 5 kilometers a day.

The wind died down by the following morning and although it was still raining and overcast, the two men retired to the bottom of the boat and Kung's mother and sister took up the rowing after they had removed the little water that had come into the badarky during the storm. This was a most welcome relief for them as they had been confined to the bottom of the boat for much of the time and had been tossed and tumbled and turned by the storm.

The two men slept around the clock, and the

mother and daughter, as they got tired, took their turns at rowing. The little girl did her best, but the bulk of the work fell to the mother who had a remarkable stamina and endurance. The next day saw scattered clouds and intermittent sunshine, and the two men took over the rowing with the same enthusiasm and optimism that they had at the start of the trip. Once again they made about 40 kilometers. By evening they saw the sea gulls and land birds that told them that on the following day they would make landfall for sure, if the weather held.

Scattered clouds came and went in the morning, and by mid-morning land was sighted. The Pilgrims moved in towards the land and saw cliffs, and rocks, and the waves smashing upon the shore. They were true men of the sea in every respect and so they knew enough to stand off a good distance in order not to get caught in the ground swells or undertows. They had learned long ages ago not to fight the ocean. If you do you will lose as the ocean is too strong. When one lives on the sea, she will supply all your needs in abundance, but she is also unforgiving and unyielding.

They read the waves of the sea as others might read a book. Soon a change in the waves told them that there was a break in the cliffs and rocks, and was letting the water go into some kind of bay or inlet. So they went as the water was going and made landfall on Sutwik Island. The first land they had seen since leaving home on Kodiak 11 days ago. They had rowed their tiny craft over 350 kilometers because the storm had pushed them to the south and they had to recover the lost distance. The actual distance from their home on Kodiak to Sutwik is only 275 kilometers.

While Kung and his father pulled the badarky up onto the shore, his mother and sister gathered some driftwood. They started a fire and soon the family was eating their first cooked meal since they had left home. They had some mussels and clams and ate some of the venison they had brought from Kodiak. After the meal, the two men went along the beach and climbed some cliffs in exploration. They soon realized that they were on an Island and that they were on its south shore. They saw no sign of life, but they saw a sheltered bay on the north side.

They returned to their badarky and that night they slept very soundly. During the night a strong wind came up out of the west, accompanied by a driving rain.

The tiny family for the most part remained inside the badarky. They only ventured out for calls of nature and to collect some clams or mussels. When they did go out, they put on the seal skin rain gear that enabled them to stay dry. Inside the badarky they had some stone lamps filled with seal oil which gave them light and some warmth. They had also brought with them some lemon grass tea which they now brewed over the tiny seal oil lamps.

The day came on with a howling wind that finally settled into a gentle breeze -- the sun could be seen off and on through broken clouds. Kung and his family launched the badarky, skirted the Island and came to the small bay they had seen on the first day on the Island. The badarky was pulled up above the high-tide mark. Driftwood was gathered and soon a cooked meal was enjoyed by a warm fire.

Once again the men went to explore and soon found several unused barabaras in disrepair. They chose one of the better ones and soon repaired it and moved in.

They planned to stay here for a week or two to resupply the badarky and get refreshed before moving on. They had just finished dinner when they heard someone outside. An old man came backing down the ladder. He was either very old or the wind, sea and weather had prematurely aged him. He greeted the family with the customary politeness and Kung's mother handed him a steaming stone cup of tea. He drank this, and then ate the food that was prepared. No words were spoken until these preliminaries were taken care of.

He then told his story. He was the Chief of Chignik village which was about 80 Kilometers northwest of Sutwik Island. With his wife and daughter he had gone out in his badarky about 20 days ago and was caught in a storm that drove them to Sutwik Island. They had made land fall at this same site. Unknown to him they had been watched landing and when he left his wife and daughter to look around two Itty-Gitty came up out of the ground.

19

He heard his wife and daughter scream. He ran back
to them, but the Itty-Gitty had already taken his
badarky out to sea with his wife and daughter in it.

At the sound of the name Itty-Gitty the hair on
Kung's neck rose and his heart beat faster. He was
truly terrified of them as were most Aleuts.

The old man continued his narrative. He had
kept out of sight in the tall grass and watched his
badarky from the shore as it skirted the Island and it
came into a little hidden cove 15 kilometers from
where they now were. He had watched the camp, and
it seemed that there were five Itty-Gitty, about six
children and about eight women including his wife
and daughter. His wife and daughter were tied and
put into a pit. They had six badarkies, including his.
Unfortunately, he had left his weapons in his badarky
and was defenseless. Two Itty-Gitty had left the camp
and headed right towards where he was watching. He
had hidden himself more deeply in the tall grass and
when these two went past him he heard them talking
about how they were being sent to kill him. They
were well armed and strong Itty-Gitty so he kept out

of their way. He had watched their camp every day and saw his wife and daughter being pulled out of the pit and beaten. It was obvious that they were not going to cooperate very easily. He had hoped that all five Itty-Gitty would leave to hunt for him after the first two had returned empty handed. So he could go down into their camp and release his wife and daughter, He then planned to take a badarky and return to Chignik for some of his hunters and come back and clean out these Itty-Gitty. He didn't have this opportunity, however, and as he watched the camp, he started to try to make weapons, but got no further than just making some primitive tools.

Three Itty-Gitty were near by looking for the Chief when Kung's family arrived, so they rushed back to their camp for help. Although Kung and his father were only two men the Itty-Gitty wanted to play it safe. The Chief rushed over here to warn them and get some weapons if he could. He was sure that all five Itty-Gitty would attack Kung and his family in the morning and, thus, give him an opportunity to save his wife and daughter. Most Aleuts were terrified of the dark so he did not think that they would attack until morning.

Kung's father gave the Chief a stone knife, several spears, and some tools and wished him luck. Although it was a moonless night and very dark, the Chief set out at once for the camp of the Itty-Gitty.

Kung, his mother, sister and father went down to the badarky and as silently as possible got it into the water. Then Kung's father took some weapons and hid behind a big boulder as a guard, where the badarky had been beached. The rest of the family went to work and reloaded the badarky in the dark. His mother and sister got into the badarky to wait. Kung was on his way to get his father when he heard the sound of a fight.

His father sensed, rather than saw, someone crawling towards the place where the badarky had been and soon he could make out two forms. His first spear caught one of the Itty-Gitties in the throat and killed him instantly. His second spear caught the other Itty-Gitty in the stomach. Kung's father then finished him off with his knife. When Kung arrived the battle was over.

These two Itty-Gitty came for the badarky at night sure that the family would all be sleeping in the barabara. The other three Itty-Gitty went to the barabara to kill Kung and his father and get the women and supplies. Even if Kung and his father had escaped from the barabara they would have been stranded without their badarky. Now Kung and his father rushed to the badarky and were soon safe out to sea. Kung and his family were certain that the great and good Agoo-Gook was looking out for them and had sent the Chief from Chignik for the sole purpose of saving them from the Itty-Gitty.

In the pre-dawn Kung and his father saw two other badarkies apparently following them quite closely. They were relieved to recognize the Chief of Chignik. As he pulled alongside, they exchanged stories. It happened just like the Chief had hoped. All five men had gone out of the camp, and he went in while the women and children slept. He had to kill two of the women who tried to fight him. He got his badarky, and his wife and daughter.

The second badarky that soon came alongside them had two women and three children in it. These women had been taken prisoners in the same manner as the Chief's wife and daughter. One of the women was from Cape Igvak with her two children. Her husband and her father had been killed by the Itty-Gitty while they slept overnight on Sutwik Island. The other woman was from nearby Cape Kuyuyukuk. She, her husband and one child had been stopped by the Itty-Gitty while they fished. The Itty-Gitty at first had been polite but when they came closer they killed her husband instantly and took her and her child prisoners. The other four women with three children, didn't want to leave.

The Chief and the two women had destroyed the badarkies in the camp which left the Itty-Gitty stranded on Sutwik island.

This little flotilla of three badarkies now made its way toward Cape Kuyuyukuk which was the nearest village. The women were strong and the Chief's wife relieved him at the rowing. As usual during the night, either Kung or his father would sleep while the other one rowed.

The overcast sky that had caused the darkness of the night before was unbroken. The next day the rain fell constantly. There was little wind and so the group made good time. By noon they were in sight of land, and made landfall at Cape Kuyuyukuk village. The woman that had been saved from the Itty-Gitty was given a hero's welcome. Few, if any, ever returned from the Itty-Gitty. It was explained, however, that because Kung and his family were on their way to the Sacred Tree that Agoo-Gook gave her and her child back to her relatives and brought her home to her village.

When Kung saw the daughter of the Chief from Chignik his heart almost stopped. She was the most beautiful girl he had ever seen. She was 14 years old with raven black glossy hair, eyes as black as her hair, a high forehead and a body that was just starting to fill out. Her salmon-berry-red lips opened easily into a bright smile and showed a set of pearl-white, even teeth. As she came out of her father's badarky, she and her mother went right over to thank

Kung and his father for helping them to escape. She took Kung's hand, her face glowing with a bright smile that showed her strong, even white teeth. Kung just about passed out with the stirring of an emotion he had not experienced before. Stammering he told her that helping them was nothing, He wanted to continue to hold her hand but also felt that he was holding onto a red hot stone. He let go and was immediately sorry he had done so. The girl's mother was saying something to him that he didn't even hear, so he politely excused himself and got away. The girl's name was Vasa, and she was the only child of the Chief.

Kung and his family were invited to stay in a vacant barabara with the Chief of Chignik. That evening they were all invited over to the central meeting barabara to tell their stories to the village people. Kung could not understand his feelings. He wanted to sit near Vasa, yet, he wanted to be far away from her. However, he had no say in the matter as the protocol of the village was such that the guests had to sit in the privileged seats reserved for them. First the Chief of Chignik, next to him, Kung's father, then the

Chief's wife, Kung's mother, then himself and next to him was Vasa.

The Chief of Chignik told his story with explanations and actions. He acted out the whole story from the time he left home until their safe arrival in this hospitable village. His audience sat spell bound as he talked and acted the rowing his badarky, hiding in the grass, and finally killing the two women who attacked him. When he finished, Kung's father told his side of the story but he did it through song, dance and gestures.

Then the conversation turned to the Itty-Gitty. One of the elders of the village explained through song and dance how the Itty-Gitty came into being. When a person in the village committed a crime against the social order of the village and refused to obey the laws, he was brought to trial and his peers would pass sentence. If the crime warranted death, the criminal was immediately killed. If the crime was of a lesser degree, the criminal was sent out of the village with only the clothes on his back. Therefore criminals of this type became known as Itty-Gitty.

The word Itty-Gitty in the Aleut language means "outside man". To live they would band together and raid a village when the men of the village were out hunting, stealing the weapons they needed, plus women and children. When the hunters would return home they would follow the Itty-Gitty and they would eventually see them in the distance, standing on a hill. They would appear to be 10 feet tall. Then suddenly they would disappear completely so it was thought they had magical power. Parents would tell their children to be careful when they went out or the Itty-Gitty would get them. Of course this was based on fact. In this way, the Itty-Gitty grew into a legendary and mythical being.

Now it was determined that these were just criminals on Sutwik Island and must be dealt with. Two of them had been killed by Kung's father and one of their own women who had been taken captive now confirmed that these truly were just wicked men and had no special ability except to beat up women.

A war party was organized to embark for Sutwik Island the next day and clear the area of these pirates once and for all. The Chief of Chignik was to lead the war party since he knew the camp of the enemy. Kung, feeling the eyes of Vasa on him, stood up and said he would follow the Chief. Twenty men were to go early the next morning and, depending on the wind and weather, it would be a four-day or five-day trip.

The meeting broke up and the two families, who now had a common bond, went to their barabara to sleep. As was the custom they all took off their clothes in the barabara. Kung, who was accustomed to seeing naked women, was somehow moved differently as he watched Vasa disrobe. He had lived in the barabaras all his life and everyone took off their clothes when they came in from outside. Therefore, Kung was confused as to why this one girl made him feel so differently and even made him conscious of his own naked body. Kung dropped off to sleep and dreamed of Itty-Gitty and how he came to the rescue and saved Vasa from the most impossible situations.

The morning dawned calm with a heavy fog over the sea and landscape. The fog was so thick that it was impossible to see more than four or five feet away. These seafaring men gave no thought to the weather and launched their badarkies. With two men in each one, the war party was made up of ten badarkies. Kung was the first rower in a two man badarky and his companion was another lad of 19 named Ookig. Ookig was down in the bottom of the badarky. The badarkies were launched about 12 feet apart, but the fog was so thick that Kung could not even see the bow of the badarky he was in, nor the bedarky on his right nor the one on his left. However, he could hear the steady swish of the paddles as they smoothly cut the water.

The rowers made good time after they cleared the breakers on the beach. About the time the sun was almost at its highest point, the fog began to clear and in a short time all ten badarkies were clearly visible. It was a most amazing feat of coordination and navigation. In what is called a pea-soup fog with no compass or other navigation aid, these men had rowed together for over six hours towards Sutwik Island in a straight line. When they did clear the fog, not one of the badarkies in the flotilla was out of line.

For untold generations these Aleut people had navigated the seas. It was the source of life for them, and they have evolved a sense of navigation that is even truer than a compass, which can be influenced by sun spots and magnetic storms.

As the fog lifted and rolled away, the flotilla came out into a bright, clear, sunny spring day with only a warm breeze that set the sea into silver shimmering ripples. The lifting of the fog and the warmth of the sun reinvigorated the war party. With only a change of rowers from time to time their progress was steady and uneventful. When night descended, millions of stars cascaded like a waterfall across the heavens. A full moon came out a little later and lit up the night with its silver brilliance.

The war party now took on the appearance of a ghostly crew, in ghostly badarkies sailing across a ghostly sea. The only sound was the swish of the paddles and the soft ripples of the sea splashing against the fast moving badarkies. These badarkies were all small one-hole, one-man crafts. They were very light made of whale bone and sealskin. The speed for these was slowed somewhat by carrying two men instead of one.

The war party made the trip of fifty kilometers from Cape Kuyuyukuk to Sutwik Island in less than one day, which previously took Kung and his family over two days,. They did this because they had almost a calm sea, no head wind, light badarkies and strong, hardy rowers.

As soon as they sighted Sutwik Island as just a black silhouette on the distant horizon, Kung took over as the leader, since it had been decided to land the group at the spot where he and his family had made their first landfall on the Island. This spot was thought to be far enough away from the Itty-Gitty's camp to be relatively safe. The whole armada made a turn to the south, and although the moon had set and it was only by star light, Kung led them all into the inlet between the rocks. It was apparent that Kung, once he had made the trip, would never forget the way.

By the time the sun came up the whole team

was safely on the beach and the ten badarkies were pulled up above the high-tide mark. A sentry was sent up on the cliff from which Kung's father had first reconnoitered when he and his family had first landed on Sutwik Island. The sentry was cautioned to stay well hidden in the grass, because if he stood up he could be observed very easily against the skyline from very long distances away. No fire was lit and all ate a cold breakfast of dried smoked salmon since the smell of fire and smoke would give their presence away.

After breakfast a Council meeting was called and all but the sentry attended. The Chief of Chignik led the Council and everyone had their say. It was decided that the enemy camp was too far away. They would have to come in closer with their badarkies. If they were to have the element of surprise on their side, they should make their attack at dawn the next morning. It was further decided that ten men would be landed at the bay where the old barabaras were and the Chief would lead this group overland to be in position at the enemy camp before dawn to ensure that no Itty-Gitty escaped on the land side to cause future problems to innocent travelers to Sutwik Island. The other ten men in the ten badarkies would make an amphibious attack and cut off any escape by badarky to sea, in the event that the Itty-Gitty had repaired any of the badarkies that the Chief had destroyed.

Fifteen of the warriors slept and five watched. The weather held clear and the sea was almost calm.

When the full moon came up, all the badarkies and the twenty men were already rounding the Island and coming into the bay. The Chief and his ten men quickly disembarked and the other ten men were soon back out to sea in the badarkies. The Chignik Chief had given very exact directions to the badarky fleet before they parted company. Kung went with the Chief on the short trip overland, and Ookig went in his badarky.

The Aleuts were all a little frightened for two reasons. First and foremost was that they did not like going overland and preferred to be in their badarkies. Even in the daytime they seldom ventured far inland from their badarkies when they gathered berries and grass for their baskets. Everything was done as near to the shore as possible. The second reason was they all had an innate fear of the night and darkness. However, they took courage from each other and in their numbers. The Chignik Chief seemed to be fearless.

The Aleut had no watch or time piece of any kind but an uncanny ability to know. by instinct. They had agreed to launch their attack on the Itty-Gitty at fifteen minutes before the first light of pre-dawn. The badarkies were in place about an hour before assault time and the overland warriors moved into position at exactly the same time. The moon had set before this movement took place, but the glitter of stars still gave some light. Everyone knew that this camp had three Itty-Gitty, four women and three children.

About forty-five minutes before the attack, one of the Itty-Gitty got up to relieve himself. He came out of the barabara and glancing seaward as was the custom, he saw the outlines of the badarkies. He bellowed out a warning as a spear caught him in the chest and he fell over backwards from the impact. The men in the badarkies heard the cry and they moved swiftly into the shore. The men around the village moved in to kill the Itty-Gitty as they emerged from the barabara. First came the three children, wailing and crying, followed by the four women, but no men appeared. The badarkies meantime had landed, and Ookig was soon at the side of Kung.

Everyone was intently watching the entrance to the barabara but Kung out of the corner of his eye caught a movement in the shadows of a hill about five meters away and reacted with lightning speed with his spear and the Itty-Gitty cried out in pain as the spear caught him in the leg. The man was down and before he recovered he was dead from five spear thrusts. These Itty-Gitty, fearing an attack, had built a tunnel from their barabara to the hill, and if Kung had not seen him, both of them would have escaped. The last Itty-Gitty, however, had already slipped away as he was the first out. He was gone.

The women were submissive and the children were fed and soon were quietly playing.   An immediate Council was called and as the day dawned clear and balmy, it was agreed that they should set out

36

at once and get this last Itty-Gitty if they could.   The Aleuts weren't trackers as they lived their lives on the sea, but the Itty-Gitty wasn't skilled in covering his tracks and didn't even have any idea of how to go about it. The one remaining Itty-Gitty just took off running and   was naked, not even wearing any footgear. He had enough presence of mind, however, to grab a knife and spear when he left the barabara.

As the Itty-Gitty ran, the grass was bent over and soon about ten of the war party were hot on his trail. Kung and Ookig were soon in the lead.   Both of these young men were very fast on their feet and they soon had the Itty-Gitty in sight. They were gaining on him and as he tired he began to slow down. The sun was now up, and Ookig was about twenty meters in the lead. The Itty-Gitty was no more than fifty meters ahead of Ookig, when suddenly he disappeared from sight, right in front of their eyes. Kung and Ookig both had the same instant reaction of fear because of the tales told to them about the magic of the Itty-Gitty since they were babies.

However, even with the hair standing up on

the back of his neck, Kung went up to the spot where the Itty-Gitty had vanished. There he saw what had happened. The Itty-Gitty had found a long ditch that the heavy rains had cut into the soft earth. He had jumped into this and seemingly disappeared. The boys signaled the others, now gaining on them, and jumped into the ditch to continue their pursuit. What made the ditch hard to see was the tall grass and bushes that grew on its banks. The footsteps of the Itty-Gitty were plain to see in the soft mud of the ditch. In some places the overhanging brush forced Kung and Ookig to crawl on their hands and knees.

Unknown now to Kung and his companion, was that the others abandoned the pursuit when they saw Kung and Ookig suddenly vanish after they had waved to them. They were sure that the Itty-Gitty had used his magic and that they would never see the two of them again.

Ookig was once again in the lead and was slowly pulling ahead of Kung. Ookig intent on watching the foot prints he was taken by surprise when he rounded a bend in the ditch and the Itty-Gitty lunged out at him with his spear from a side ditch that drained into this main ditch. Ookig was only quick enough to turn aside and the spear went into his arm, and he fell over backwards. The Itty-Gitty fell on top of him and holding Ookig down. He was just raising his knife to finish Ookig off when Kung's spear caught the Itty-Gitty full in the chest.

The other pursuers had returned to the camp of the Itty-Gitty and had told their amazing story of how the two men had disappeared right before their very eyes. A hurried Council meeting was called, and it was agreed that they must leave Sutwik Island at once. The Chief wanted to leave Ookig's badarky behind, just in case that the two men might have survived. He was voted down because the one Itty-Gitty still alive, as far as they knew, would then have transport and could once again raid, steal and kidnap. The Chief who was very brave and thought that Kung and Ookig might still be alive said that he would stay. If the two were gone, he would deal with the Itty-Gitty before he would return to Cape Kuyuyukuk. Another brave man offered to stay with the Chief to make sure that Sutwik Island would be safe for future travelers in the area.

The flotilla was still in sight when Kung and Ookig arrived back at the camp. The Chief took Ookig in his badarky, after they had dressed his wound. Kung and the other man took the other badarky, which had been left behind with the Chief, and in less than an hour's time they were following in the wake of the homebound warriors. Since Ookig was wounded, he did not row. The weather surprisingly held clear with only a sea breeze blowing, and Kung and his rowing companion from time to time exchanged places with the Chief in his badarky so that he could rest. This was done by the Chief crawling forward from the rowing hole and Kung or his companion holding the two badarkies together. Kung would then transfer to the aft part of the Chief's badarky, and the Chief would transfer to the bow of Kung's badarky. Then he would crawl very carefully to the rowing hole and go down it. This maneuver may sound easy but it was extremely dangerous and was never attempted when the sea was up.

That night after the moon had come up, the war party was pulling its badarkies up above the high water mark at Cape Kuyuyukuk. Kung's father, mother and sister, and Vasa and her mother were down on the beach along with Ookig's family, when the news was relayed that Kung and Ookig had been made to vanish by the magic of the Itty-Gitty. Vasa's father, the Chief, had stayed behind, along with another brave soul, to finish off this last Itty-Gitty.

Vasa, of course, was worried about her daddy, but she could not keep the picture of the strong young man out of her mind. She felt a strange feeling of having lost something very precious. Also, she had felt an attraction for the strong and handsome Ookig and also felt this loss very deeply. Kung's family was devastated by this unexpected blow. How was it possible that the great and good Agoo-Gook would take away their son and brother when they were on the way to His Tree. Why had they ever stopped at that evil Sutwik Island? However, they realized that if only to save Vasa and her mother from a fate worse than death, they would have stopped. Kung's and Vasa's mothers had in the last two days grown very fond of each other.

Now as the full impact began to slowly sink in, Vasa and her mother told Kung's family not to be so sure about Kung's not being alive. "Let's wait until the Chief of Chignik returns," they pleaded. "For he is very wise and has lived long and gotten himself and his people out of situations much more difficult than this one, and if Kung and Ookig are dead, he will bring their bodies home for proper burial in the Spirit Caves." This wise and sagacious council rekindled a faint ray of hope in the bereaved family and consoled them considerably.

The two families sat up together as Kung's family was too distraught to even think of sleeping.

Suddenly, they heard footsteps, and the Chief was backing down into the barabara followed by Kung. Ookig had been taken home to his family. Everyone in the barabara started talking, crying and laughing all at the same time. Of course, the whole story had to be retold by both men to the laughter of all, when they realized that the vanishing Itty-Gitty was nothing more than a trick. Sutwik Island would now not only be safe for travelers but also for pilgrims, such as themselves, going to Agoo-Gook's Holy Tree.

-3-

The next morning the wind picked up and the rains returned. Kung went with Vasa to visit Ookig. His arm was angry red and swollen, and he had a fever. The medicine man had been in and applied his herbs and concoctions and had given him some strong tea to drink to bring the fever down. When he saw his friend, Kung, a big smile lit up his strong young face. He had told his story to his family and so Kung was received as an honored guest in this barabara. He now explained to Vasa again how Kung had saved his life.

In a few days the fever was gone, and the arm began to heal. By the end of three weeks Ookig was completely well.

In the meantime Kung and Vasa spent hours together. They went to fish camp and cleaned, smoked and dried the salmon that were now running full force in the streams and rivers. On nice summer days they went berry picking together and shared their dreams and aspirations.

The woman and her two children that had been rescued by the Chief from the Itty-Gitty had to be taken back to Cape Igvak about 125 kilometers away. Vasa's father agreed to take them to Cape Igvak before he departed for home in Chignik. The other women and children from Sutwick Island stayed in Cape Kuyuyukuk. Kung and his family had decided to await the chief's return so that they could go on to Chignik together.

Once Ookig's arm had healed, he asked Kung to go seal hunting with him and the two friends went off together. Since both men were skillful hunters, they had great luck. The following day they went salmon fishing together. Then they both decided to go to a more remote fish camp together for about three weeks.

Vasa was left behind and became despondent. She had a vague feeling of jealousy towards Ookig for taking Kung away from her. She also had a strong feeling for him and she found herself day-dreaming about the tall, handsome Ookig, who was older than Kung and seemed more the man. In her eyes he was the hero for catching up with the Itty-Gitty. At the same time and alternately, she day-dreamed about the young, kind and good natured Kung. He was also a hero in her eyes for saving Ookig's life. She also admired Kung for going on the war party with her father. She had been vivacious and felt gay and happy being with Kung. Now she missed him and began to have visions of Kung and Ookig's being mauled by one of the huge brown bears of the area, or of them getting caught in a storm and drowning, which was common among her people.

At the end of three weeks when neither her father nor Ookig and Kung had returned she began to get up at daybreak to go to a high promontory where she could see to the northeast, the direction all three men had gone. One day she saw a single badarky making its way toward her. She almost fainted with anxiety until it was closer and she recognized it was her father's badarky.

She ran down the mountain, and the two

families were waiting at the landing to meet him when he arrived. Her first question was about Kung, and her father said that in the last few days he had not seen a living soul.

Vasa was now certain that something terrible had happened to both men and her despondency grew more acute. She was not working now and spent all day up on the promontory eating dry fish, salmon and blue berries, which were now in full season. The whole village was busy with the fishing and hunting, drying and smoking fish and Vasa's parents were anxious to be on their way home to Chignik. Kung's parents were also anxious, for the summer was now almost over and they also began to worry about Kung.

The Chief and Kung's father agreed to wait for another three days and then they would go on a search party. Several of the villagers agreed to go with them since they knew the camp that Ookig was going to take Kung to.

Vasa spent from dawn to dark with Kung's sister on the promontory the third day. The sun had already sank below the sea and dusk was turning to night when the two girls saw two tiny dots in the distance. They were sure that they saw something but the night came on too fast and the two little dots disappeared into the darkness.

The two girls rushed back down into the village and they went to the beach to wait.

An overcast sky made seeing impossible. To add to the anxiety of the two girls, it soon began a light drizzle. The girls were wet and miserable and were just about to give up when they heard the swish of paddles emerging out of the night. Soon they could see two heavy laden badarkies take shape out of the dark. Kung and Ookig were suddenly engulfed by two screaming girls when they were barely out of their badarkies. Other villagers soon appeared and helped the two men haul their over-laden badarkies up above the high-tide mark.

When Vasa hugged Kung, he felt a warm feeling inside, and he acknowledged to himself that he had indeed missed this beautiful girl. He also felt a real pang of jealousy when he saw Vasa give the same kind of enthusiastic hug to Ookig.

That night in the barabara the two men explained that the fishing had been extremely good in their camp, and they just could not give it up. In fact, they had only left the fish camp because their badarkies could not carry anymore dried and fresh fish.

The Chief and Kung's father agreed that they would depart Cape Kuyuyukuk as soon as possible for Chignik.

The following morning when Ookig heard that they were leaving, he made up his mind at once to also make the pilgrimage to the Holy Tree. His close association with Kung and Kung's enthusiasm had taken hold of his heart. The two men had gotten to know each other quite well and their friendship had blossomed into a deep and sincere lasting relationship. Kung was delighted with this decision, and Kung's father and the Chief agreed that he could go along with them to Chignik and from there, they would leave it in the hands of Agoo-Gook.

It was further agreed that Vasa would go in Ookig's badarky as his relief rower. Kung did not know why, but he was not happy with this arrangement, but he said nothing. He could not understand his feelings. All he knew was that he did not like it.

The day of departure was clear and warm with a gentle breeze blowing from the south. Kung and his father were rowing, and his mother and sister were in their customary place in the bottom of the badarky. The Chief was rowing and his wife was in the bottom of their badarky. Ookig was rowing and Vasa was in the bottom of his badarky. The supplies, tools and weapons were evenly distributed among the three badarkies according to the weight and carrying capacity of each. Once again, Kung felt chills run up and down his spine at the thought of being on the way to the Holy Tree of Agoo-Gook.

Ookig's family was very happy that their son was going to the Holy Tree. The family was sure that this would bring great blessings to them, but they were also sad, and he had a tearful separation from his family and friends. All the villagers had come down to see them off, and the two families truly felt that they were leaving a second home. The people of Cape Kuyuyukuk were warm and friendly. Over the three month period they were there deep friendships had developed among them.

The weather held all that day and night. From time to time the Chief would rest, and his wife would take over. The same in Ookig's badarky with Vasa taking over the rowing. She was a strong girl, yet only a girl, so Ookig had to relieve her more often. Kung at night went to sleep and his father continued to row, and then Kung would be aroused and take over, and the father would sleep.

About noon the weather began to cloud over, and the wind shifted from the northwest, so the rowers had to buck a head wind. The seas started to pile up, and the rain started in the afternoon. The Chief, Kung and his father got into their sealskin rain gear. Ookig felt the rain and cooler wind and he was glad to cool off, and did not tie himself into the badarky sealskin. However, he soon realized he had made a mistake, because as the seas got bigger it took all his skill and strength to just keep his badarky into the wind. There was no time to put on his gear or seal up the badarky. The waves as they washed over the tiny craft sent some water each time down the rowing hole to Vasa and soon she was laying in cold sea water but dry, since she had earlier put on her sealskin rain gear and checked all the supplies in the bottom of the badarky to make sure that they were properly sealed against the water.

Ookig realized that the badarky was taking in water and that he and Vasa would drown if he did not seal up the hole. He waited until a wave that did not seem as large as the others bore down on him. Then swiftly, with no lost motions, he got into his sealskin gear. He then righted the badarky back into the wind. On the next small wave he attempted to tie the rain gear up, but he was too slow, and the next wave caught him broadside and the third one flipped him over.

Vasa was terrified. The sea water was rushing in, and the badarky was upside down in the high seas. Ookig was strong and skillful, and in less than a minute he brought the badarky back right side up. The cold dunking and the increased adrenaline flowing in his veins, gave him the strength and clarity of mind he needed to save the situation. He was once again bow first into the wind. His sealskin shirt was tied halfway. Vasa now was still dry, except for her face, but the cold water chilled her to the bone. There was no escape for her nor for Ookig. No more water was coming in, but Ookig did not dare to chance another flip, so he could not finish tying up his shirt and each wave that washed over him drenched him from the waist up.

Kung and his father saw what happened and so did the Chief. Kung's father signaled Kung. Kung took full control of holding the badarky into the wind while his father went aft. Kung then guided his craft in front of Ookig's, and the father tied a line to the bow of Ookig's badarky. Once Kung's father was secure back in his hole and his sealskin in place, he signaled the Chief and he came astern of Ookig's badarky and Ookig went aft and secured the Chief's badarky to the stern of his craft. Now it was Kung's turn to go forward and let out the sea anchor. This was a perilous undertaking but was done with dispatch and skill. Once Kung was back in his hole and the sea anchor was holding the three badarkies into the wind, Ookig and Vasa were able to bale the water out of their badarky. Vasa would fill up the jar with water using a large clam shell and then pass it up from the bottom through Ookig's badarky shirt. He would empty it and pass it back. This process was repeated until the badarky was once again free of water.

The storm was short-lived, but the seas remained high. However, about mid-morning Kung was able to take in the sea anchor. The three badarkies remained tied together, and by evening the seas had abated enough to allow Kung's mother and sister to take over the rowing and get some fresh air. The rain had stopped and the sun was breaking periodically through the clouds. The Chief's wife was also rowing and so was Vasa while the men were all able to get some needed rest after the grueling ordeal of the storm-tossed night. That night the wind shifted back to the south, and the three badarkies were separated once more.

The rest of their trip into Chignik was uneventful. The weather cleared and the days were warm and sunny and the people in the badarkies enjoyed themselves and best of all there were no mosquitoes, which on land were a constant irritation. The three badarkies made land-fall in the afternoon and a big welcoming party was planned for that evening. The Chief gave Kung and his family their own barabara, and Ookig was invited to stay with them.

That evening was a repeat performance of singing and dancing and story-telling of their struggles and great adventure. Vasa sat between Kung and Ookig, and there was a warm feeling of closeness between all three. They laughed when Ookig showed and told them how the Itty-Gitty had disappeared, and they looked at Kung with new respect as Ookig explained how Kung had saved his life. The best part was when he reenacted and told the story of the near-capsizing of his badarky. Everyone laughed until tears rolled down their cheeks. Everyone knew the gravity of the situation, but Ookig was a master story teller and actor. He used facial expressions and body language to show the terror on Vasa's face and her lying in the cold water. It was hilarious and the near-tragedy became the talk of Chignik.

Vasa had turned fifteen and was soon to go through the purification ceremony that marked her coming into womanhood. This ceremony was held at the fall equinox and again at the spring equinox. Kung's parents were anxious to be on their way, but the Chief and his wife prevailed upon them to stay. It was agreed that the summer was too far gone to make Umnak before winter, and it would be wise and prudent to winter here in Chignik where they had a barabara and close friends. Only the great Agoo-Gook knew what conditions they would encounter for the winter if they went on.

Life in the village of Chignik was much the same as life in most of the Aleut villages. The women and men all worked at catching, smoking and drying salmon. The men made new badarkies and repaired the old ones. The women wove their watertight baskets from special Aleutian grass, picked berries, herbs and dug roots. All gathered clams and mussels and carried out the multitude of tasks required by the social order of the Aleut culture.

The education of the children started at birth. It was the duty of everyone to teach the children. The little girls and boys learned to be mothers and fathers by helping to care for the younger children. By the example of their parents and neighbors they learned how to be husbands and wives.

When a child would see someone weaving a basket and come and pick up the dried grasses, the weaver would stop and most patiently teach the child the art of weaving. When the child tired of this game, it would go over to watch the man chipping the stone or whale bone to make weapons. This craftsman would stop and patiently teach the child how to choose the best material and shape it into the best weapons. So it went for every profession in the village. When a child showed a special aptitude for something and had the desire to perfect it, the villagers would devote all their years of experience to train this child to be the best and encourage it to even try to improve on the quality of what they chose to do.

There was no such thing as private property in the village. For example, if a man was a real craftsman at making spears his pay was to see the leaders and best hunters go to the spear rack and choose his spears. The same was true of the builder of badarkies. This was not true however of visitors. Kung's family's badarky and Ookig's, it was understood these were theirs and was to be left alone so that these visitors could leave any time they wanted. When a visitor saw his badarky being taken he knew that he was a prisoner of that village.

As the lush green of the hills and valleys began to change to a dull brown as summer gave way to fall, Vasa, Kung and Ookig now became inseparable. These two men did not understand what was happening. Vasa was extremely vivacious and filled with energy, and she flirted with both men all the time. The result was that both of them fell in love with her and, in spite of their deep friendship, they became jealous of each other and were constantly vying for her attention.

Vasa, because she would be eligible for marriage after the purification ceremony, was in all of her maiden's glory. Not only did she have the devoted attention of Kung and Ookig but some of the other young men in the village as well. She played the game for all it was worth. She was flirting with all the eligible men around her.

-4-

The day of the purification ceremony was a beautiful sunny fall day. Vasa's old clothes were taken off and burned. She was then taken into the village steam bath and rubbed down with sweet smelling herbs. The water used to make the steam on the hot rocks was also sweet smelling. This aroma soon permeated the whole village.

The two old women assigned, as they massaged her young body chanted prayers to Agoo-Gook to guide and protect her, to help her be a good person, to find her a good husband, to be a good wife, to help her to have healthy children, to be a good mother and a good neighbor to all in the village. They had her pray with them that she would always follow in the right ways of Agoo-Gook. She was then dressed in new clothes and sent to the mountain above the caves for the dead to pray, fast and meditate.

Those in the caves who had gone on into the

spiritual world would come to her and advise her on the course of her life. She was to stay on the mountain until she was given this spiritual guidance. This ceremony also gave them needed strength of character to face the problems and vicissitudes of life.

The first day on the mountain she smelled the smells of the sea, vegetation and flowers. She felt the warmth of the sun, and was contented and happy. That night, however, she became terrified and was unable to sleep. The gentle breeze of the day turned into the voices of the spirit world at night. She even imagined that she could see these spirits taking shape by the light of the star-studded sky. She also had visions of the wicked Itty-Gitty that had been killed on Sutwik Island, and who had held her and her mother prisoners, coming to capture her again. When the sun had finally turned to a rosy dawn, she was exhausted. She fell into a deep and dreamless sleep.

This sequence was repeated the second night and added to her terror she was also thirsty and famished. The third night she dreamt senseless and meaningless dreams.

The fourth day she awoke to a light drizzle and overcast sky, but was warm and dry in her rain gear. She began to pray to Agoo-Gook in earnest.

She began to think deeply about her future and thought a lot between prayers about Kung and Ookig. She also thought about the other young men she had known since childhood, who were now her suitors.

That night she did not pay any attention to the night sounds. She kept to her prayers and finally fell to sleep. She had warm furs and sealskin covers to keep her dry.

In her sleep she had a dream of a very bright light that turned into a man as it came close to her. He said that He was the light of Agoo-Gook, and He assured her that she was safe. He was surrounded by a heavenly light. Love, kindness, compassion and understanding flowed from Him to her. He told her in three days He would return, and she would know the path she must take to accomplish the goals of her life. He was gone and Vasa slept out the night in a dreamless, deep sleep.

The next morning the sun shone brightly and the hunger, thirst and terror she had felt were gone, but she was still tired and she prayed and slept and prayed some more. A new calm seemed to come to her and she felt an inner peace she had never felt before.

She came to find a new mature understanding of her girlish flirtations, and she was sorry. She asked Agoo-Gook for forgiveness. She realized that surely all of these men but one would be hurt now by her rejection of them. As the realization came to her, she began to pray for them and forgot all about herself. That night and the next day she prayed only for others, her mother, father, Kung's parents, Ookig's parents and she even prayed sincerely for the spirits of the evil Itty-Gitty who had captured them.

The third day after the first visitation of the light of Agoo-Gook, she woke up refreshed and not in the least tired. She washed herself and fixed her hair and prayed most sincerely and waited. All day she waited and nothing happened. As the sun was about to plunge below the horizon she began to feel pangs of disappointment. After all, it was only a dream. Just then she saw a mist rise up out of the distant sea and come toward her. She rubbed her eyes and thought maybe she was dreaming again, but, no, it came on and soon turned into the brilliant light of her dream and it came to rest next to her on the mountain. The same man of her dream emerged and told her that she must always have faith in Agoo-Gook and never doubt. As long as she followed in His way, He would be looking after her in His spiritual world. She must trust Him completely, this was the only safe path through life. His parting advice was to look at everything from the eyes of Agoo-Gook and not from her own. He was suddenly gone.

Vasa seemed to awake from a trance. She had swooned and was laying on the ground. The night had closed in.

The next morning Vasa came down from her mountain, She was a woman, and a changed woman.

She tried to see with the eyes of Agoo-Gook and everything was more beautiful than she had ever seen it. All creation from the rocks, to the flowers, to the animals, to the children, all were beautiful in a most dazzling way. She even felt that the sun was warmer, the breeze more gentle and the smells more aromatic than she had ever experienced. She also felt a deep spiritual love for all creation, but most of all for Agoo-Gook.

Now as she thought of Kung, Ookig and the other young men she knew and felt that only Kung was totally devoted to Agoo-Gook. Ookig also was going on the pilgrimage to the Holy Tree, but he had been encouraged and led to do so by Kung. Ookig was the tall and handsome one, and he was also very brave and a good hunter. He had proven himself to have a superior sense of humor. He was good-natured and was a gentle and kind man. So from the physical standpoint he was the best catch and would be the better husband. However, by seeing with the eyes of Agoo-Gook, she chose Kung because of his innate spiritual qualities. He was to be her man and no other. Her mind was made up.

Vasa went looking for Kung only to find that he, Ookig and some of the other men of the village had gone on a whale hunt about three days ago. They had gone towards Perryville.

At night Kung and Ookig had some heart-to-heart talks around the campfire about the seemingly fickle Vasa and all her flirtations. These were thoughtful and reasonable men, and as they talked they came to the realization that Vasa was flirting and intentionally leading them on and playing them off against each other. If they let it continue, they would destroy their wonderful friendship. Thus, it was agreed between the two friends that Vasa would have to make her own choice and the courting of the two friends with her would stop.

If she wanted one of the men from Chignik, so be it. This decision took the pressure off the two men, and for the rest of the hunt they were more relaxed and had a wonderful time.

The whale hunt was carried out in a very different kind of boat than the one or two man badarky. It was an open whale boat. It was also made of whale bone and sealskin but it held about twenty men. Three or four men were in the bow and each had strong spears. These spears were fastened to a long line made of sealskin leather. The end of the line was securely fastened to the whale boat. When a whale was sighted, all the men would carefully track it and when the whale surfaced for air, if they were in position, they would let fly with their spears. These spears had a barbed point that went in easily but would not come out.

It was the morning of the fifth day out that the whalers spotted their first whale, but when they saw that it was a female with a new-born calf they gave up the chase. That afternoon another whale was sighted and the hunt was on in earnest. All four spear throwers in the bow made their casts, but only two spears penetrated the thick hide deep enough to hold. The whale sounded and the exhilaration of the boat being towed at break neck speed through the water by the whale was very exciting. When the whale surfaced the second time to blow, the whale boat was too far astern to make another cast. This happened because so much line had to be let out so that when the whale sounded to avoid being pulled under the water by the whale.

After the whale made its second run all twenty men began taking in line only to let it out again when the whale sounded into the deeps. On the third surfacing, to blow the whale boat was near enough for the spear men to make another cast. This time all four spears took hold, making six spears in the animal. Now it was just ride, let out line, take in line, be towed and wait.

The whale began to tire and the men would come alongside when the whale surfaced and drive the spears deeper into its body. This went on for three days and three nights through rain and sunshine. The men took turns sleeping in snatches. At the end of the third day, the whale surfaced and died. The prize was theirs. Now came the laborious task of towing the whale back to Chignik. All twenty rowers took up this task with one will. They were bone weary and exhausted but jubilant with this catch that would assure the village of ample food through the winter.

It was two weeks since the men had left. When they returned and beached the whale at high tide, the whole village turned out to butcher it. Every single part was used, nothing was wasted. Then it was time for a feast and a celebration.

Vasa found Kung in his barabara ready to collapse. She decided it was not a good time to tell him about her spiritual experience on the mountain. Kung was polite and, yet, somehow Vasa sensed a difference. This worried her. He seemed distant. She thought it was because of his physical exhaustion, yet it still worried her. The next day she was kept busy with the other women preparing the feast. She saw Kung off and on, but he made no attempt to talk to her.

That evening at the feast some of the other young men that Vasa had been flirting with came to her. As usual she expected Kung and Ookig to come also but they did not. Her heart was heavy. She was polite to all the suitors but she let them know that she was not at all interested in them, and soon she was sitting by herself.

Then she saw Kung and Ookig talking and laughing with two other women about her age, and it was her turn to become jealous. She felt deserted and rejected just when she was so sure of herself and her future with Kung.

Vasa had a lot of backbone and courage and she knew that anything worth having was worth fighting for. She left the feast early and went home. Kung and Ookig saw her send away all the suitors and then leave. This set them to wondering what had happened to her.

The next morning she fixed her hair with extra care and then went directly to Kung's barabara. He still seemed distant, yet, he was polite, but she was not to be put off and asked him to go for a walk with her. He made some vague excuses, but she told him that it was important and about Agoo-Gook. At this, his curiosity was aroused and he agreed. As the day was cool, clear and beautiful, they walked along the beach and she recounted her experience on the mountain at her purification ceremony. Kung listened with rapt attention. As she talked about the spiritual light he thought he could see something about its reality by looking at her. She was glowing as she told her story. When she got to the part about her deciding to marry him because she saw and felt something of his spiritual nature, she became shy and felt that she was being presumptuous. She didn't even know for sure if he cared enough about her to want her for a wife. She went on anyway and told him of her feelings and her decision. Kung stopped walking and looked deep into her eyes. She blushed and looked down to the ground and was quiet. Suddenly, she felt his two strong arms around her, and he drew her to himself and lightly kissed her on the mouth, and then he began to laugh as he took her hand and led her on down the beach.

He then related the talks that he and Ookig had at the campfire on the whale hunt. She agreed that what she had been doing was very childish and asked him to forgive her. Again he drew her to himself and gave her another gentle kiss and told her he had nothing to forgive. They then went back to the village and packed up a lunch and headed for the mountain where Vasa had her spiritual experience. They spent the day praying, talking, kissing and hugging.

That evening Kung went to Vasa's mother and father and asked for permission to marry her as was the custom. Then Vasa and her mother, father and Kung went together to Kung's parents for their permission. These families were already close. So Vasa's parents were delighted at the prospect of having such a wonderful strong, courageous and spiritual son for a son-in-law, and Kung's parents were equally delighted at having such a lovely woman for a daughter-in-law.

The wedding was arranged for the next full moon. As Vasa was the daughter and only child of the Chief, it was to be a gala affair. Her family also agreed that she was to go with Kung to the Holy Tree the next spring. It was also agreed that after the pilgrimage, Kung and Vasa would return to Chignik and spend some time with Vasa's family before returning to Kodiak.

Then Vasa and Kung sought out their friend, Ookig.   At first he thought that Kung had deceived him. When vasa told him of her experience on the mountain and Kung further explained how Vasa had come to him, not he to her, which was the center of their agreement, Ookig accepted the outcome good naturedly.

Vasa's father gave them a vacant barabara. It was a good one, but was in need of extensive repairs. Ookig came over to help when he could, and Kung's sister came daily to help Vasa prepare her first home. It was a happy time for everyone with a lot of laughter and joking. As was the custom, Vasa and Kung went to the community meeting house for the things they needed, remember that in their culture they had no private property. Vasa made some new sea otter fur clothes for herself and her man, and she also made up a new outfit for their friend Ookig.

On the day of the wedding, some of the old women came to visit Vasa. They told her what to expect that night and each was full of sage advice that they passed on to Vasa along with a lot of joking and teasing. The same was done with Kung, with the elder men of the village. This advice was based on what the elders before them had taught them, plus what they had gained from their own life time of experiences.

The wedding was a very happy one with a lot of story telling, dancing and singing. Kung was now eighteen years old and Vasa was fifteen. Ookig, was nineteen and for him not to be married was a rare exception among the Aleuts. Ookig however said that since his true love Vasa had married his best friend, he would never marry. He said this with a twinkle in his eye.

The wind, rain, snow, sleet, ice and high and low tides all came and went. Life went on in its settled way with hunting, fishing, fixing tools and weapons, mending clothes, making pots and weaving baskets. The peace, serenity and warmth of the winter was only broken by the arrival of a stranger who claimed to be from Kodiak. This stranger had no way of knowing that Kung and his family now living in Chignik had only last spring left Kodiak. They knew the man was lying and so they did not trust him. However, he was made welcome and given food and shelter in Chignik. That night as everyone slept he went to the warehouse and stole tools, weapons and supplies and a good strong badarky, the one he had arrived in was almost useless.

This would have been overlooked by the villagers and they would have just let him go, except when he left he had also stolen a young woman.

Ookig, who was still staying in the barabara with Kung's family, was awakened by what he thought was a scream. Ookig went outside to investigate and as the night was clear with a half moon, he was able to see the stranger forcing the young woman down into the bottom of the stolen badarky. He had now tied and gagged her. Ookig rushed back into the barabara, quickly dressed, grabbed his weapons, and while he did this, he explained to Kung's father what he had seen. Ookig did not wait for comments or help but ran to a badarky with his weapons, pushed it out to sea and was in hot pursuit of the stranger and his captive.

Kung's father roused the village and soon ten badarkies were on the trail behind Ookig, including the woman's husband and her father.

The stranger was no match for Ookig, and with his stolen plunder and the woman, his badarky was too heavy. Ookig was gaining on him with every stroke of his paddle. The stranger, realizing he could not get away, got out of his hole and was trying to pull the woman out of the badarky to dump her into the sea, as a last hope of getting away. The woman was not cooperating. She had guessed his intentions. Ookig came along-side, and as the man was lying on top of the badarky with his hands groping for the woman in the bottom, he was in no position to fight. Ookig's spear caught him in the side as he tried to raise up and he fell into the ocean. Ookig asked the woman if she could move. She recognized Ookig's voice, but she was still gagged and she could not answer. She came up out of the bottom of the badarky and Ookig removed her gag and cut her bonds.

Suddenly, Ookig felt his badarky was filling up with water. The stranger, though seriously wounded, had pulled the spear out of his body and had thrust it several times into the bottom of Ookig's badarky. The stranger then swam towards the stolen badarky the woman was in, in order to stave it in also. Ookig saw what was happening, and using his paddle, he hit the man on the head, with all his might.

The man let go of the spear and slowly sank out of sight. Ookig told the woman what had happened and that his badarky was sinking. Ookig passed over the weapons to her and she paddled her badarky in next to his. He then, carefully so as not to upset her badarky, transferred himself to her badarky. She then went back to the bottom of the badarky and Ookig went into the hole and started rowing towards Chignik. He was soon met by the war party that had set out in pursuit of the stranger, and they all returned to Chignik together.

That night Ookig performed the whole

episode in song and dance to everyone's delight. Ookig had become the most famous actor in Chignik, not only for his acting, but was famous for his courage and strength. He was respected and admired by all. This was especially true of Vasa and Kung.

The winter days were short and the nights were long but they were often shown the brilliant night sky, of the north, lit up with the Northern Lights.

As the brown hills started to turn into emerald green and the snow beat a daily retreat up the mountain sides, Kung and his family decided to get on with their pilgrimage to the Holy Tree of Agoo-Gook. The day they chose for departure dawned cool but clear. Only a slight northeasterly wind was blowing. This time Kung had a one hole badarky and Vasa was to be his relief rower. Kung's father, mother and sister were accompanied by Ookig as the relief rower for the heavier two man badarky.

The first day they only made about 2 knots per hour because they had to buck a slight head wind and some heavy seas had built up. The next day the slight wind went down somewhat and they made about 3 knots per hour. Everyone was in excellent health from the hunting and daily work load in the village over the winter. Plus they had a good and plentiful diet. In the beginning, Kung would spell Vasa after only a few hours of rowing, but by the second day she rowed for a straight six hours while Kung slept. The larger badarky with Kung's parents still followed the same pattern, as it did on the trip from Kodiak.

In the warmth of the day with a spring sun chasing the snow up the slopes of the distant mountains, Kung's mother and sister got out in the fresh air and did their stint at rowing. Morning and evening both men rowed. Then after dark they took turns sleeping and rowing. At midnight the two badarkies anchored offshore at Perryville. The wind had tired of blowing, and with the calm that followed a thick fog settled over Perryville and the waterfront.

The pilgrims were welcomed with traditional Aleut hospitality in Perryville. Everyone in the villages up and down the Aleutians felt that the great and loving Agoo-Gook would bless them by how well they treated pilgrims that came and went to the Holy Tree. Some of the Perryville people had friends and relatives in Chignik, so greetings were exchanged. Vasa even had an aunt and uncle and some cousins who lived in Perryville. As was the custom the pilgrims were assigned a barabara. The fog burned away as the sun came up, and it was a calm and beautiful day.

That evening at story time, Ookig reenacted the story of the Itty-Gitty with some added embellishments to make it more interesting and humorous. It was late at night when everyone retired after an excellent show.

The next day was devoted to resting. The travelers were anxious to get on and take full advantage of the exceptionally fine weather. The weather held clear, calm and sunny and so the following day, the group bid goodby to their hosts in Perryville and were underway at day-break.

It was late afternoon when Kung spotted some badarkies coming out of Ivanoff Bay. He pulled alongside his father's badarky to talk and they decided to avoid contact, because they had heard rumors in Perryville about a band of pirates operating in this area. After the consultation, they moved away seaward, but it soon became obvious that there were five badarkies and they were definitely in pursuit. Kung's group would face some problems in defending themselves. First, their badarkies were heavily loaded and second they had been rowing all day and were tired. Kung's badarky was a single-hole badarky, so he went ahead. It was easier to fight from the two hole craft-- one man could fight while the other rowed. They still tried to avoid contact and put all they had into their rowing.

Two of the pursuing badarkies steadily gained on them and Ookig, who was in the front hole, placed his weapons on the bow of the badarky. He was to be the rower and Kung's father, who had the most experience, was to be the fighter. Kung was advised to keep going and under no circumstances was he to turn back. If they lost the battle they might lose by only one bedarky. The other might have a chance to get away.

Kung's father turned round facing backwards in the bedarky to face the enemy. He laid out his weapons on the stern. He knew that he would be in trouble if the two badarkies came at him at the same time.

One of the badarkies was in the lead, however, and it was apparent that the man was over confident. He was the stronger as his rowing proved, and he was anxious to take the prize. He was also experienced and knew that he had to get in close to make his kill. Kung's father used this to his advantage. As the pursuer was coming on fast, he stood up, which was totally unexpected by the enemy, and with all his strength, let fly his spear. It was a long distance, but by standing up he was able to do it. Even at that distance the spear almost went through the chest of the pursuer. In the meantime the other badarky which was close behind came on. Kung's father had almost fallen out of the badarky when he threw the spear and his upper body was sprawled on the stern.

The second fellow threw his spear at Ookig. He knew if he got Ookig out, he and the other four badarkies, which were still some distance back but coming on fast, could win the day. He was broadside of Ookig and an easy spears throw away, but Ookig saw him. Just as he threw the spear, Ookig put on the brakes with his paddle and the spear just went in front of him. The next two strokes of his paddle turned the stern to the foe. Kung's father had regained his balance and with another spear, in one motion, killed the second enemy, before he could rearm himself. The two men now took off behind Kung and did not wait for the other three enemy badarkies to catch up. The other badarkies when they caught up with their dead friends and saw what had happened, lost heart and the fight was over.

The rain returned with some wind. Sometimes a head wind and sometimes a tail wind, so the rowing went on. It was the morning of the fourth day when Unga Island was sighted. Landfall was made at Sandpoint around noon. Again, the pilgrims were received with warm hospitality. That night Ookig gave his rendition of the encounter with the pirates of Ivanoff Bay. As usual the show was appreciated by all. In the consultation that followed, the men of Sandpoint decided that they would take a war party to Ivanoff bay and deal with the pirates.

The next day, twelve badarkies took off for Ivanoff Bay, with the shouts and encouragement of everyone. That afternoon the wind picked up, but it would be a tail wind for the war party. Kung's group felt that they had enough of fighting so they did not join the war party. The weather stayed bad and the wind howled and screamed and the waves crashed on the beach. The group had been given a barabara and everyone was snug and warm below ground, while the tempest raged above them.

The unrelenting weather screamed and thundered for two weeks. The pilgrims helped with the work of the village and repaired their clothes, weapons and tools, and waited. The beginning of the third week the storm began to lose its strength and in a few days the rain stopped and the sun came out. However, the pilgrims could not leave as the seas still crashed and thundered as they tore at the beach. They would have to wait until these high seas generated by the storm subsided.

The Sand Point war party that had gone to Ivanoff Bay returned and reported that the villagers of Ivanoff Bay had been unaware that they harbored some pirates. The five badarkies of young hunters that had gone out on the day in question, when they returned with two of their friends dead, they told the villagers that they had been attacked by a war party of ten badarkies from Perryville. Which had killed their two friends. The other three had managed to escape.

When the Sand Point war party arrived the villagers of Ivanoff Bay were putting together a war party to go attack Perryville to avenge their two dead sons. When the war party of Sand Point explained what the pilgrims had told them about the incident, the elders of Ivanoff Bay called a Council meeting. The three young men were questioned separately. When they were asked how they happened to escape with the dead bodies of their friends, the three gave different answers. When one of them was pressed, he confessed that over the past six months, for fun and excitement they had been going out and attacking any easy prey. They had been successful until they had attacked Kung's party. They thought five against two would be a pushover and had regretted getting their friends killed.

The village Council was divided. Some wanted to just send them off as Itty-Gitty. The others wanted to just put them to death. They argued that if they sent them out they would just continue in their evil ways and kill and hurt others in the future. The Aleut had no jails, no prison system, so the options for punishment were very severe. It ended up that the three men were given to the Sand Point war party for their trouble. They could keep them as slaves, kill them or make them Itty-Gitties.

Now the war party had returned with their three prisoners. They were all tied together and paraded through the village. The people of Sandpoint wanted to give them to Kung's father as slaves. Kung's father was saved from this burden by the fact that his family and Ookig were on their way to the Holy Tree.

The sun shone through broken and scattered clouds and the seas calmed sufficiently for the pilgrims to leave Sandpoint. As was their custom they set out at first light in the morning. They picked up two more badarkies of pilgrims at Sandpoint. One was a family of five. The oldest child was a girl eleven, the same age as Kung's sister. The boys were aged nine and eight. The family also had a two-hole badarky, and they had been underway for two years. They came from Karluk on Kodiak Island, and Kung's mother knew them from childhood.

Also joining them were a couple, a man about twenty and his wife about nineteen. This couple had been married for five years and had no child. They decided to go to the Holy Tree and ask Agoo-Gook for a child at that sacred place. The couple came from lower Ugashik Lake and had been underway for just a year and had wintered in Sandpoint.

The small flotilla got underway and again the weather held steady, clear with only a slight sea breeze. The fishing lines were out, and from time to time they would catch some fresh fish. They ate the fish raw, but occasionally they cooked the fish over the seal oil lamps in the bottom of the badarky. This cooking was a problem as the lamp and cooking caused a smoke, and those in the bottom suffered from it. Also it could only be done in the calmest weather, as fire on the badarky meant death for sure.

The fourth day the little group arrived in Belkofski and by now the red salmon were running. Everyone stopped to work, catching, smoking, and drying fish, in order to supplement their whale meat, seal meat and other fish that they had started out with.

They spent two weeks between Belkofski and King Cove where the fish camps were.

The badarkies of this area were constructed differently. They used the same material and the same style hole, but they were outfitted with outriggers. That is they had a balancing pole fitted to one side. Those badarkies with outriggers could not be turned over and in this way, no matter how rough the sea became, no rower need be dunked in the icy water. The sea was becoming colder as the water from the Bering Sea was cooling off the Pacific waters. Kung's father and Ookig decided to use this feature of outriggers on their badarky, but Kung did not want to carry any more weight or create any more drag so he did not put the outrigger on his. The other two followed the lead of Kung's father and modified their badarkies.

The childless couple really took to the children and, of course, the children responded to the extra love and care that was showered upon them. The man was playing and teaching the boys every spare minute. The woman did the same with Kung's sister and friendl.

The children's mothers' and fathers' were delighted at this turn of events as it gave them some respite from the three active children. Kung's sister and the other little girl quickly became fast and firm friends, bonded together by the pilgrimage and by being traveling companions.

The weather again closed in. The storm continued to rage for five days unabated. The pilgrims could do nothing but wait. They all sincerely thanked Agoo-Gook for settling them in at Sandpoint and Belkofski during these fierce spring and early summer storms. All were sure that His spirit was indeed looking after them, for they knew it would take a miracle to survive out to sea in this type of storm.

When the storm finally calmed down, the intrepid travelers in their frail crafts, once more put out to sea. This time they were not so lucky. The next day after departure an east wind picked up and the they got their first taste of the famous Aleutian willow-wa. The wind was blowing hard and steady from the east when all of a sudden, sounding like the roar of many thunders, came a fountain of water out of the west pushed by a wind of at least twice the velocity of the wind from the east. This is what creates the willow-wa. Fortunately, for the pilgrims the tide was running with them. However, the first willow-wa passed about a hundred meters away from the nearest badarky, but the second one caught Kung's badarky square on and he was instantly flipped upside down . He was tied in and no water got in as he righted the badarky, but it was a chilling experience. Then Kung's father's badarky was also hit, but it only got spun around, thanks to the out-rigger they had installed. With the tide and the east wind pushing them, they moved along at a fantastic speed.

These men of the sea learned quickly, and in a short time were able to anticipate the path of the willow-wa and were able to maneuver out of its way. The rain came in a torrent accompanied with lightning and thunder. However, their tiny badarkies climbed up each mountain of a wave, and like surfboards went skimming down the other side. They had to keep the badarkies lined up with the waves. If they did not they would get a broadside and a freezing cold shower at the least. Kung got flipped upside down each time he was not perfectly lined up in his badarky. Now he realized that the out-rigger was necessary in this part of the Aleutians. After the third dunking, he vowed that he would not venture out again on this sea without one.

After dark the storm did not seem to be letting up at all. The little armada of badarkies edged into the shore as close as they dared to go. They sensed, rather than saw, a tiny sheltered cove with a sand spit over which the seas from the east were breaking, and they made landfall in the cove on the west side of the spit. The shore was rocky but everyone helped and unloaded the four badarkies. They all had water-tight seal-gut rain gear and stayed dry in the torrential rains. They helped each other get the badarkies up above the high-tide mark, and all settled into their badarkies for the rest of the night.

When the wind picked up in the morning the badarkies were weighted down with stones, but still they shook and trembled in the wind.

The crew was trapped in this small cove for three days before the wind began to settle down into just a strong wind. They were still trapped for two more days before the seas subsided sufficiently for them to even consider going on.

Kung, his father and Ookig used the two days waiting time to rig an out-rigger on Kung's badarky. The wind was still from the east and the days were warm and sunny. Mosquitoes, were the problem now on land. The mosquitoes came in hoards, if anyone even opened their mouths mosquitoes would fly in.

Now the tide began to change and would be running toward the west and with the wind out of the east also pushing so the pilgrims went back to sea. The greatest relief was to be away from the mosquitoes. The travelers had already passed False pass in the night when the storm started and they now decided to go on to Akutan about 175 Kilometers away. They decided to make landfall as needed on the changing tide.

They were now in the area where the tides would be going one way and the wind in the opposite direction, thus, creating fierce tide rips. So they would go with the tides and land before the tides changed. If they did not, the tides would carry them backwards no matter how hard they rowed, and they would be expending themselves for nothing.

The fleet of four badarkies ran with the wind and the tide. With this push they were moving at between ten and twelve knots. As the tide slowed and before it began to run in the other direction, the four badarkies would be landed, and moved above the high water mark. Then they would wait the next tide change to move on again. The wind held strong and steady. The next run was as good as the first. On the second day the smoke from Akutan Volcano was sighted and by evening they were into Akutan village.

The pink salmon were now running, and the salmon berries were ripe. The weather held warm and sunny and the Aleuts of Akutan were warm and friendly. Since most of the people from Akutan had made the pilgrimage to Umnak and the Holy Tree, some good friendships were made, and the village elders gave advice to the pilgrims. They were cautioned about their runs through Akutan, and Umnak Passes. It was explained that the most dangerous parts of their pilgrimage would be going through these passes. They were also advised that once through the passes, they should hold some distance off-shore as the winds and willow-was were most dangerous when combined with the ground swells in close.

While they were in Akutan fishing and berry picking the unexpected happened. Ookig fell head-over-heels in love. She was a little woman of eighteen and not yet married. Like Ookig, she never felt just right about anyone. Her name was Annik.

Also in Akutan there was a big Aleut of twenty, the same age as Ookig. He was a head taller than Ookig and about 25 kilos heavier. His name was Stevng. He was the bully of Akutan and did not hesitate to whip into line anyone and everyone that crossed his path. He also was a handsome fellow and considered himself the Don Juan of Akutan. Of course, he was madly in love with Annik. She for her part couldn't stand the fellow, but even if she had liked someone in Akutan, he would have been scared off by Stevng.

At the evening story telling time, Ookig put on his full show of the Itty-Gitty and each time he did it, the show was enhanced by his additions. It was truly a work of art and tears of laughter rolled down the people's faces. Annik was swept off her feet by this tall handsome man, and as she also had a keen sense of humor, she appreciated his acting, dancing and singing. Ookig then did the show of the pirates of Ivanoff Bay. This was given an ovation by the whole town.

Then all turned to honor Kung's father. They were awed over for his skill and courage in facing the five badarkies single handedly. Well, almost single handedly, as he did have some help from Ookig, which Ookig failed to bring out in his acting and story telling.

Every day Ookig would be out with Annik to fish camp, or berry picking or what ever. Stevng could not just sit by and let this go on.

THE FIGHT

-6-

One morning as Ookig came out of his barabara, Stevng challenged him to a fight. He made it a public challenge, in front of the whole village, so that Ookig could not refuse. He accused Ookig as an outsider who had come to Akutan and stolen his girl. Now Annik was very fearful of this happening, and she had warned Ookig about Stevng. Ookig had laughed it off. He had never been afraid of anyone, not even the Itty-Gitty that had almost done him in. Stevng was sure that Ookig would not be man enough to face him in a fight. If he were, he would crush him in body and spirit in front of the whole village. To Stevng's surprise, Ookig laughed in his face in front of the people who were outside. He accepted the fight. It was to be a no-holds-barred fight with no weapons, and they were to fight until one or the other called it off. Kung's father and one of the elders of Akutan were to supervise.

The fight became the talk of Akutan, and the plans went forward for the day of the next full moon.

98

Almost everyone in Akutan was sure that Stevng would win, including Stevng.

He had been brawling and bullying others since he was a child. He had never lost a fight in his twenty years of fighting. He fought almost daily. Annik went to Ookig and told him that all this fight would accomplish would be the exaltation and fame of the bully and Ookig's getting beaten up. She said that they should slip away together.

Ookig laughed and kissed her and told her not to worry. It was true that he had not fought a real fight, but he had been on a number of war parties and as a child he had practiced with a skilled teacher. They both went to Annik's parents and asked for permission to marry. The girl's father told Ookig that he was agreeable to the marriage but his permission would have to depend on the outcome of the fight. He did not want his daughter to be known as the wife of a loser. This just gave Ookig the added incentive to put an end to this bullying once and for all. Ookig's, pilgrim companions could not leave now until after the fight.

When the fight began, Ookig took over at the very beginning. Stevng rushed in to overwhelm Ookig. Ookig sidestepped and slammed his fist into Stevng's kidney as he went past, and Stevng fell flat on his face on the ground. Stevng was big and heavy, but Ookig was quick and nimble on his feet. Stevng had never before been knocked down and now in front of all these people, how could this be? He jumped up and with a roar and both arms swinging wildly he came in again only to be caught square in the nose by Ookig. Blood gushed out and this seemed to clear Stevng's head. This time he came in alert and cautious, but Ookig this time caught him in the knee with his foot and Stevng was down again. If only he could get hold of Ookig, he would break him in half. As if Ookig could read his mind he seemed to let Stevng grab him, but all of a sudden Stevng found himself flying through the air and he hit the dirt on his back. What kind of man was this he was fighting? This time Stevng found it more difficult to get up. Ookig waited and did not even try to come in and finish him off. It was almost like a cat playing with a mouse. Yet, it was not in Ookig's nature to torment someone. This time when Stevng came in, Ookig caught him full on the jaw with a powerful uppercut, followed so fast by a powerful right cross and Stevng was out cold before his body hit the ground.

From the start, all the men that had been beaten and bullied by Stevng were shouting for Ookig to kill him. Now that Stevng was out and beaten, everyone went wild and headed for the promised celebration. Annik was glowing with pride and happiness for her man. Annik's father was already bragging to his friends about his wonderful son-in-law. Ookig was not even breathing hard.

Stevng came back to consciousness slowly. He was all alone, and he realized that he had been truly beaten by a smaller man in front of the whole village. As his head cleared, he knew that his position was gone forever in the village. The only way to redeem himself and regain his position of leadership among the other young men was to kill Ookig.

He also knew that it had to be a fair fight. The laws of the Aleut and Agoo-Gook were very strict. If he killed Ookig in any way except in a fair fight, it would be murder and he would be instantly put to death. He also knew in his heart that he would rather be killed by Ookig than have to live with this stigma for the rest of his life.

The party was in full swing with laughing and dancing and story telling when suddenly Stevng was standing in front of Ookig. He threw Ookig a knife and then raised his own. Every person in the barabara moved away from the two men. Ookig knew the situation instantly, and told Stevng that this was not worth dying for. Stevng snarled back that yes it was, and he lunged at Ookig. Ookig easily side stepped, and with his knife handle in his fist he brought it down on the back of Stevng's neck and Stevng was out cold for the second time.

This time the elders and the Chief of Akutan came forward and sincerely apologized to the visitors. They took Stevng outside and securely tied him to a stake. Then they all agreed in Council that it would be better if the visitors would leave Akutan as soon as possible. They all felt that Stevng would come to his senses in a few days.

That same night Annik and Ookig were married.

The next morning, at the crack of dawn, the four badarkies plus one new one, with Ookig and his bride headed toward Biorka Island on the tide. There was only a slight warm breeze blowing, and the day came on clear and sunny. With Kung and his wife in one badarky and Ookig and his wife in another, this left Kung's mother and father to row their own badarky. Kung's mother was strong like her husband and son and was able to take turns, with the rowing as good as the men. The badarky was also lighter for the provisions had been distributed according to the capacity and weight of each badarky. All the badarkies were fitted with outriggers.

The trip from Akutan took two days and as they approached Biorka island about thirty badarkies came out fast and surrounded the pilgrims. There was no escape this time, and they were escorted into the village at spear point. Ookig's wife, from Akutan, was recognized, and the others identified themselves. The villagers of Biorka Island profusely apologized, but explained that they had been at war with the Aleuts of Unalaska and Amaknak for twenty years and they dared not let their guard down for a moment. They never knew when the next attack would come.

To explain the Biorkan's actions, the story was told that twenty years ago there was a family in Biorka that had nine sons and one daughter. This daughter as she grew up became the most beautiful woman in all the Islands. She was also gentle and kind and was always helping the old people, the children, and the sick. She always had a kind word for everyone. Her mother and father doted on her. Her brothers adored her, and because they loved her so much and wanted to keep her for themselves so they did not want to let her marry. She was happy with this because there was no one she wanted to marry. To protect her, the family decided to move out of Biorka to the other side of Beaver Inlet on the

mainland of Unalaska Island.
The family with ten men and two women were quite prosperous and happy.

One day the daughter was picking blue berries up on Biorka Pass, which is between Beaver Inlet, where her family had settled and the village of Unalaska. All of a sudden a very handsome young man from Unalaska, who was also picking blue berries in the Pass, was at the same blue berry bush. They began to talk, and he was as sweet and kind as she was and the inevitable happened--they fell in love and made a pact to meet in the Pass as often as they could. The young man wanted to go to her parents, but she dissuaded him from this folly. She explained that her brothers would surely kill him if they even found out that they were meeting, let alone in love.

These clandestine meetings went on for some time, and the woman got pregnant. The brothers became suspicious and followed her. When they saw her with this man they knew what had happened. They were furious and determined to put her lover to death. The daughter, however, overheard them talking, when they thought she was asleep, about how on the next meeting they would lay an ambush and slay this upstart from Unalaska village that had the temerity to even touch the most beautiful woman in the Aleutians.

The next day when the men went seal hunting, the woman left her home and went over Biorka Pass to the village of Unalaska to her lover. She warned him that her brothers and father planned to kill him and that they must get away.

The young couple were married and left for pilgrimage. No one ever saw them again.

The brothers came home and realized that their sister had run off to Unalaska and to her lover. They immediately went over to Biorka and told their friends and relatives that their sister had been kidnaped by the Unalaska people. They were believed, and a war party was organized to go to the village of Unalaska and rescue the woman. Of course, this war party fell on the unsuspecting villagers of Unalaska. They came over the Biorka

Pass so the Unalaskan's were caught unawares, for no self-respecting Aleut would go overland if he could help it.

The Aleuts from Amaknak Island and Unalaska Village retaliated. When friends and relatives are killed their deaths must be avenged. The Biorka Island Aleuts kill any Unalaskan they catch and vice-versa. Although from the prisoners they captured both sides eventually learned the truth. The brothers and their mother and father had long since been killed, and the feud continued and no one knew how to end it. The Unalaskan and Amaknak Island Aleuts have more warriors and are stronger, but the Island of Biorka is built like a fortress and so it is easily defended. There are very high insurmountable cliffs all the way around with only one small cove to land in.

Kung's father came up with a brilliant solution. He suggested that their Chief of Biorka and some of the elders go to Umnak to Agoo-Gook's Holy Tree. Warring and killing are forbidden on the Island of Umnak under Agoo-Gook's law. When Kung's father would get to Unalaska he would make the same suggestion to the Chiefs and elders of Unalaska and Amaknak. Then on that sacred ground they could arrange a permanent peace, things could be settled and the raiding and killing stopped. The people of Biorka thought anything would be worth a try. The biggest problem was to be able to sneak past Unalaska Bay without being caught by the Unalaskan's or the Amaknak Islanders. In any event, it was worth a try. Then the elders began to make plans.

The weather seemed to be holding so the next morning the five badarkies took to sea. They had the tide with them and it should have been an easy passage. However about 10 Kilometers into the Pass out of Beaver Inlet, a head wind came up, blowing from the northwest against the tide, thus creating some big tide rips. When the wind increased, the tide rips became like waterfalls or cliffs of sea water bearing down on their tiny bedarkies. These tide rips and mountainous waves smashed into the little fleet. They tried to make a run for the shore, but the whale bone ribs cracked like toothpicks and ruptured the sides of the badarkies. Kung made it to shore with Vasa, but his badarky was beyond repair. He found his mother and father bruised but alive. Their badarky was also smashed and torn. Then they found Ookig and Annik also badly beaten up and their badarky in ruins. They also found the young man and wife alive. Then they saw the other family's badarky. It was still at sea. The waves had subsided some, and it looked like the children were trying to paddle the badarky into the shore. The man who had grown to love these children did not even hesitate and jumped into the freezing water, swam out to the badarky, climbed in and brought it safely to shore. The children's mother and father were not found.

They had one badarky left out of five, and it was damaged. The young couple from lower Ugashik Lake that were going on pilgrimage for the sole purpose of praying for children took these children as their own. Most of the tools, weapons and supplies had survived the ordeal because of there water proof wrappings. So the other four damaged badarkies were all brought together and a camp was made. Fortunately, the storm passed as quickly as it had sprung up, and the wind died down.

The whole crew turned out to work and they stripped down the four damaged badarkies. They began to repair Kung's father's badarky first, since it was the least damaged, using the whale bone and sealskin from the most badly damaged one. All that was required on the children's badarky was to fix a few cracked ribs and some tears in the sealskin. This was quickly done. This gave them two two-man badarkies. They were able to repair, but poorly, one of the one-man badarkies. It was decided to cram Vasa, Kung's mother and sister into the bottom of his father's badarky, which was built to have only two people at a time in the bottom, with Kung and his father as rowers. the three children were put in the bottom of their badarky with the young couple as rowers. Ookig and Annik were in the one man badarky, with Annik in the bottom and Ookig as rower.

The repairs had taken four days. On the fifth day the rain came, but they caught the tide anyway and they rounded Priest Rock into Unalaska Bay with no further problems.

Unalaska Bay is a very large bay. It is on the north side of Unalaska Island. The mouth of the bay is from Priest Rock to Eider Point. Within this bay is Morse Cove, Summer Bay, Captains Bay, Ruffs Bay and the whole Island of Amaknak. There are numerous coves, inlets, islands and beaches in Unalaska Bay. It is known as the best protected and the largest bay in the Aleutian Islands.

At Morse Cove they saw fire on the beach and landed at a fish camp. Again, the villagers recognized Ookig's wife from Akutan and the group was warmly received. This camp had a whale boat from Amaknak. They took the pilgrims in the whale boat the next day into the Village of Unalaska. The families were given barabaras up in Captains Bay, at the mouth of Pyramid River. The pink salmon were still running and everyone went to work, to catch, dry and smoke fish.

The pilgrims decided that they had better winter here. This was the most sheltered bay in the Aleutian Chain, fish and game were plentiful and they could rebuild their badarkies. Umnak and the Holy Tree were now on the next Island. The first Pass had proven equal to its reputation. Now there was still Umnak pass ahead of them.

Kung's father met with the Chiefs of Amaknak and Unalaska and their Councils to discuss the Biorka problem. They were also sick of the feud and all the killings and raids. The resentment and mistrust toward the Biorka people ran deep. Kung's father was a master diplomat and so the elders and the two Chiefs finally agreed to go to Umnak and at least talk to the people from Biorka in order to save the lives of their own kin and their people if possible.

As the pilgrims waited out the winter to continue their journey to the sacred tree they were kept busy. They went with the villagers on a whale hunt that was very successful and three whales were brought in that winter. The herds of sea lion came into the bay when the weather turned cold. Meat was plentiful with ducks and geese added to the menu. Halibut, shrimp, king crab, dungeness crab, tanner crab, octopus, squid, clams and mussels were plentiful. Unalaska has a saying that when the tide is out the table is set.

Ookig's story-telling talent was recognized and he was in demand all around Unalaska Bay. When he didn't have a true story to tell he used his imagination and made one up. Vasa and Annik became the closest of friends. Sometime in April both women became pregnant. Vasa was now seventeen and Annik was nineteen. When their pregnancies were announced a big celebration was planned. Ookig and Kung were as inseparable as ever. The young couple from Ugashik Lake now had three children to love and care for.

The badarkies were completely rebuilt and new ones made. New fur-seal clothes, and new seal gut rain gear were made for everyone. All the pilgrims spent a happy and productive winter up in Captains Bay.

It was a warm spring day and twenty badarkies rounded Eider Point headed for Umnak and Agoo-Gook's sacred Tree. The Chief of Amaknak was in a two-hole badarky with two relief rowers in the bottom, and the Chief of Unalaska was outfitted in the same manner. There were another eight one hole badarkies for the elders. Each had a relief rower in the bottom. Then, there were the four badarkies of the original pilgrims. A young man who had wanted to make the pilgrimage took Kung's place in his father's badarky. In another four badarkies were folks who had come into Unalaska on their way to Umnak and who now joined this group. The last two were from Makoshin and were going home.

These men of Unalaska and Amaknak could read the ocean like others read books. They could forecast the weather accurately from the signs in the wind, sky and sea. On the second day, they rounded into Makoshin Bay and where the volcano was almost asleep with only a white vapor streaming off into an azure blue sky. The hills were already turning into a brilliant green. The only snow left from the winter could be seen on the slopes of Mount Makoshin.

The visitors were all well-received and a huge celebration was arranged for the next day. Most of these visitors had relatives and friends living in Makoshin Bay, which was almost as heavily populated as Unalaska Bay. It was seldom that so many distinguished guests came together. The Chiefs met together with the Chief of Makoshin and his Council. They decided that the Makoshin villagers should also lend their support to the peace effort at the Holy Tree, and five more badarkies were assigned to go with them.

Another ten badarkies joined the group as they departed two days later from Makoshin Bay.

At Kashiga village, their next stop, another three badarkies joined them. This made a flotilla of 31 badarkies. When they arrived at Chernofski, the weather was still holding with a light wind, blue sky and no sign of bad weather. However, the elders from Unalaska and Makoshin agreed that they should not attempt to cross Umnak Pass because a violent storm was in the making. There were not enough empty barabaras in Chernofski to house so many people, so they made do with their badarkies out in the open. The travelers from Unalaska, Makoshin, and Kashiga began to tie their badarkies down with big boulders, lines and stakes. Kung and his group decided to follow their example although there was not a cloud in the sky or a trace of wind, just a gentle breeze was blowing out of the south.

In the late afternoon the breeze shifted and came out of the northwest and began to pick up speed. It seemed like only minutes later that the sky had turned an inky black and the rain came down like a waterfall, but pushed by the force of the wind it came horizontally. The wind had now reached the pitch of a screaming, howling monster. The willawas pushed up geysers of water over 50 meters high. The waves thundered and crashed upon the shore, and the noise of the storm made conversation impossible inside the battened down badarkies. This storm raged and howled for three days non-stop, after which it began to quiet down. The storm became just a normal violent Aleutian storm for another week. At the end of two weeks, the sun began to peep through the clouds, and the wind shifted back to the south.

Several badarkies that had not been properly

battened down were damaged and needed repairs which were made with dispatch. The elders from Unalaska Island refused to budge and, sure enough, the following day another storm came in this time from the north. It was short-lived, however. The following morning all awoke to the blue sky once again and a slight easterly wind.

This time the elders prepared to go at the best possible tide, which was slack tide. Instead of going west, they led the flotilla of badarkies at a southerly angle across the Pass. As the tide began to flood they were all well out in the Pass, and the tide swept them north at an incredible speed. They went sweeping out into the Bering Sea like chips of wood caught in the cross currents of a mighty river. They were far enough into the pass so that as the tide pushed them out into the sea they were on the Umnak side. The leaders now led the armada well off from shore. In fact, they were so far out in the Bering Sea that you could just barely see Umnak Island in the distance. Kung and his group remembered the advice they had gotten in Akutan about staying well offshore. They were also very thankful that the kind Agoo-Gook had

sent them these wise seamen of the Aleutian Passes to
see them safely across.

-8-

At the west end of Umnak Island, the Holy Tree came into view. Once again every man, woman and child felt the rushes up and down their spines. Many wept openly. How could such a Tree grow where no other could? How could it withstand the forces of a storm like the one they had just experienced and not be uprooted and thrown to the ground? Surely only the power and force of Agoo-Gook could have achieved it.

There were probably close to 5,000 badarkies on the beach, and if there were only two occupants to each that would mean at least 10,000 people. The people were circling the Tree and praying. A sweet love and peace pervaded every atom of the place.

On the first day Kung and his party met another family from Kodiak that had been here for a year and were now going to head for home. They had a barabara about a kilometer away, and when they left they told Kung's father that he could have it. It was a long way from the beach and would mean packing their things this distance, but all decided that this would be better than living any length of time in the badarkies.

There were more Aleuts living on Amaknak and Unalaska Island, but they were scattered from Beaver inlet on the east to Chernofski on the west. Just in Unalaska Bay from Eider Point to Priest Rock there were probably close to 10,000 Aleuts. From Kodiak to Attu, including the Pribilof Islands they probably numbered over 100,000. Umnak Island was the only place, the whole Aleut nation considered their Holy Land. Here they came to thank Agoo-Gook for his blessing, to seek His guidance, and to help them to understand and achieve their purpose in life.

The fourth day after their arrival, the Chiefs of Unalaska, Amaknak and Makoshin came to Kung's father and asked him to locate the Chief of Biorka and his elders. They asked him to act as their representative to set up face-to-face talks. This he agreed to do. But, the Chief of Biorka was no where to be found. Kung's father, after a week of looking and asking questions, finally gave up.

It was obvious that the Biorkan Chief and elders had not come. This was confirmed by some of the pilgrims he did meet from Biorka.

The friends leaving for Kodiak departed. The barabara they left was a very large one, yet with all of its room it could not accommodate ten people. Ookig and his wife stayed in the badarky. The young couple with the children found some friends who had room and moved in with them.

The Chief of Biorka and his elders arrived the following week. The Council held its meetings in Kung's father's barabara. In the atmosphere of peace generated by the spirit of the Holy Tree, it was impossible to remain hostile. In the main the Aleut people were of a peaceful nature and soon a strong and abiding peace pact was agreed upon. What was past, was past and all agreed to try to forget and forgive.

Once this peace pact was concluded, the

Chiefs were anxious to return home. The weather now was holding them on Umnak. In fact, when the storm came, many of the people had planned to depart. Summer was coming to a close and some of the people wanted to get as close to home as they could before the fall storms would come.

The morning after the storm had spent itself and the sky cleared a most strange thing happened. Everyone at the site of the Holy Tree awakened to find two strange badarkies on the horizon. These badarkies were huge. They had what looked like many very white sealskins on trees that grew out of the decks. Many men could be seen on the decks. When they got closer to shore, the men could be seen up in the trees folding up the white sealskins.

Soon from each badarky three large whale boats were lowered. Ten men in each boat and six boats they rowed ashore. All the Aleuts were on the beach to welcome these new guests that had come to pay their respects to the great Agoo-Gook.

These were the strangest people anyone had

ever seen. Their skin was pale. They also had blue, brown and grey eyes. Their hair was not black but brown, red, and even yellow. The same for the hair growing on their faces.

The Chief and his elders of the Holy Place went forward, as was expected, to greet these strange new-comers. They spoke a language no one understood. The man who seemed to be in charge made signs that they wanted food and water. The people all went and brought what they could. The leader pointed to the big badarkies and repeated many times "ship". The people quickly understood that the big badarkies were called ships. The sixty men that had come ashore quickly filled up large wooden kegs with water and some of them began to transport the food and water to the ships. Some of the Aleuts returned to their prayers around the Tree.

One of the whale boats when it came ashore again, had some strange-looking men on board who were wearing long robes with things on their heads. These men asked questions that no one could answer because the strangers did not speak in the Aleut

123

language. They then went to the Tree, but they did not show the proper respect. One of the Aleuts tried to show them that they must bow down when approaching Agoo-Gook's Tree. One of the pale men hit this man on the head with what looked like a stick, but it was not a stick. Everyone could not believe what they saw for all people were taught from birth that violence of any kind was forbidden by Agoo-Gook on the whole Island of Umnak. These men with the long robes watched the Aleuts around the Tree, pray and worship in the prescribed way. The robed men talked together for awhile. Then one of them went to the whale boat that was returning to the ship and said something to the men on board. What he said was, "Look at these stupid people worshiping that stupid tree. We must destroy this Tree. Please bring several axes on your next trip and we will cut it down and save these ignorant savages from hell."

When the axes arrived, several men started to attack the Tree, at the direction of the robed men. Now the Aleut had again been taught from birth that this Tree was a gift from the great invisible Agoo-Gook. They were commanded by the voice of the

Eternal to take care of the Tree, and He would be their Agoo-Gook and they would be His people. The Aleuts tried to take away the axes, but the men from the ship pointed the sticks, which were not sticks at these Aleuts. They made a sound like thunder and the Aleuts fell over dead. The cry went up, "They are killing the people on forbidden ground, quickly to your weapons. We must save the Tree." The Aleuts scattered in every direction to fetch their weapons that were stored away.

Kung, Ookig, Vasa and Annik had gone out to the hills for a day of berry picking and were unaware that these ships had arrived. When the ships appeared they were on the other side of a hill. Their first intimation that something was happening was when they heard the first shot. They rushed to the top of the hill and saw the strange ships for the first time but they were too far away to see what had actually happened at the Tree.

Ookig had a bad feeling. He suggested that they approach the area of the Tree with extreme caution. The four kept to the tall grass and gullies that ran down the hill and got to about 500 meters from the tree. When the Aleuts scattered, the huge pale-colored men retreated to the whale boats, but did not attempt to go back to their ships. All of these men, except those in the long robes, had the thunder sticks in their hands.

Now the Aleuts, men, women, and children with spears, knives and rocks, came back in front of the Tree. The thunder sticks roared and many Aleuts died but the spears and rocks flew and some of the men from the ship also died. The thunder sticks roared again and more Aleuts died. Kung and the others emerged from the grass just in time for him to see both his mother wounded and his father killed. The angry cry of the Aleuts swelled, and with one accord they advanced on these strange creatures that dared to violate the Sacred Ground. The sixty men pushed off in their whale boats as the Aleuts advanced, and they continued to shoot volley after volley into the crowd.

The beach was covered with the dead, dying and wounded. Only about 10 of the strangers were killed and another 5 were wounded. By the time Kung's group arrived it was all over. The strangers had returned to their ships. Kung's father was dead, shot in the face at close range, and his mother was dying. Kung and Ookig were carrying his dying mother to the barabara when the ship's cannons let go at the crowd still on the beach. They had filled the breach of the cannon with chain links and shot and people died by the thousand. People scattered screaming in every direction. The ships fired one more salvo at the retreating Aleuts, killing several hundred more. Then the cannons fell silent. Death and destruction were everywhere.

Kung's mother died before they got her to the barabara. The body was left with the women, and Ookig and Kung went back to the beach to look for his sister and bring back his dead father. The dead were scattered everywhere. They found the Chief of Unalaska dead alongside the dead Chief from Biorka. Most of the Chiefs and elders had been killed since they had been the ones in the front. They found Kung's sister and her little girl friend both dead in the grass, killed by the cannons. They had been hit in the back with shrapnel as they fled. His sister was holding a rock in her hand. She had been with his mother and father trying to save the Tree. The other little girl's foster father was found searching for her. He, his wife and the two boys were safe.

It took all of Kung's strength to keep going, but his father had to be brought and his body prepared for burial. The nearest burial caves were a day's rowing from here.

A War Council had been called and Kung and Ookig had to go. Kung was thankful now that their barabara was so far from the beach. This gave the women at least a little security. The War Council was split right down the middle. Half of the men said that even if they would be all killed, they should not raise their hands in violence as Agoo-Gook had forbidden it on this Island. The other half maintained that Agoo-Gook had commanded them to take care of the Tree, and even if they were all killed they should die like men, defending Agoo-Gook's Holy Tree.

Ookig pointed out that with these strangers'

big ships, cannons and guns, fighting with them would just cause more people to die and this would be useless. Ookig reasoned that the only way for now, was to retreat, and try to learn about their weapons. If Aleuts could get their thunder sticks and could learn how to use them then, they might stand a chance of saving the people. This argument was rejected out of hand.

Kung was too grief-stricken to care. He had lost the people most dear to him in this one day. All he had left in the world was Vasa and their baby yet to be born. He was also confused about Agoo-Gook and His Tree. If Agoo-Gook was indeed an all powerful creator, why didn't He save the people that had made such sacrifices to come all this way to worship Him? It was His Tree, and if He wanted the people to save it and look after it, why didn't He supply the knowledge and the means to do just that?

That night under the blanket of darkness, Kung, Vasa, Annik and Ookig in two badarkies, towed Kung's father's larger badarky with the bodies. They slipped out to sea, headed for the burial caves.

The following morning they carried the big badarky up into one of the caves and faced it towards the sea in the opening of the cave. They used the dry grasses to preserve the bodies and placed his little sister in the bottom of the badarky with her little friend. Then, in the front rowing hole went his mother, and in the back one went his father. Food, weapons and tools were left in the badarky to see them safely into the spiritual world. They all said their prayers, and asked Agoo-Gook to escort them safely into His special home.

While the burial was going on, they could hear the shooting of the guns and booming cannons, and they knew that more Aleuts were dying. They decided not to return to the Tree and left the caves saying their farewells to their loved ones. They headed out into Umnak Pass the following day on the tides and made a safe crossing into Chirnofski.

During the next two days, a steady stream of refugees arrived from Umnak. The news was all bad. The strangers had attempted a number of return landings, and each time they were driven back into their ships by the Aleuts, but at tremendous cost for the Aleuts. The thunder sticks, or guns as they came to be known, took the lives of many Aleuts. Only a few of the strangers were killed or wounded. Their guns were more effective at greater distances than were the spears of the Aleuts. They would come in just out of range of the spears and shoot any Aleut that appeared. Men women and children were killed in this way, it made no difference to the strangers.

The group of Aleuts that arrived in Chernofski left together. Those from Unalaska were now bound together by a common tragedy to even those from Biorka. They made Kashiga, and learned that the news of the tragedy had already reached there. The same was true at Makoshin when they arrived. Every place they were organizing war parties and dispatching them to the Tree. Kung and Ookig tried there best to dissuade the forming war parties, telling them that it was folly to send their men to be killed as they would stand no chance against the enemy's superior weapons.

They described the situation at the tree, and this was verified by the other refugees. The reply was universal, "It would be better to die defending the Tree of Agoo-Gook than to die of old age." Of course, they could not see or imagine the death and carnage that the refugees described. Nor could they be convinced that they would not be able to defend their Tree under any circumstances.

When they went back to their barabara in Captains Bay on Unalaska Island, it was like a ghost village. Some of the women had moved back with their parents on Amaknak, some to Makoshin and some, to Unalaska village, while their men-folk went off to save the Tree.

Kung was a completely changed person. It seems that he had grown old over-night. He spent long hours climbing up Pyramid Mountain by himself. However, Vasa was a realist and her child would be born in the winter. They must have furs, food, and the barabara in good condition. In a gentle way, she made her needs known to her husband. Kung loved his wife now as intensely as when he first married her, and so he began to share his thoughts with her and Ookig. He felt it was only a matter of

132

months or maybe even weeks before the strangers with their ships would come to Unalaska Bay. He felt it would not be wise to antagonize these men further. Ookig agreed with this for the time being.

Kung and Ookig now turned their full attention to providing for their families. The silver salmon were running full and the seal, and sea-lion were plentiful. The men also built another hidden barabara up behind a little hill some distance away from the village and stocked it with dried meat and fish. They were fearful that if the strangers came they would take all the supplies, and their families might starve.

It was during this time that the war parties came back from The Tree. The young man, his wife and the two little boys also came back. The returning people reported on how the ships had prevailed over them. More than 5,000 Aleuts had been slaughtered. The Tree was cut down. The men in the long robes were called priests. These priests saw how the Aleuts still came and put their heads down on the ground at the Tree's stump and wept. They asked Agoo-Gook to forgive them because they were unable to defend His Tree and take care of it.

These priests decided that the new name of this place should be "Nikolski" and they built a building made of wood on top of the ground near the Tree stump. As explained the Aleuts lived under ground. They made the Aleuts work day and night on this building. If they got tired or sick they were beaten. If they made any sign to defend themselves or their families or their friends the defenders were shot. One of the priests began to learn a little of the Aleut language and he told the people what to do.

One of the Aleuts killed one of the priests and the men from the ships killed ten Aleut men. The Aleut who killed the priest was taken aboard one of the ships and for a week his body hung from the ship's mast.

The building was called a Church and the strangers said that the true Agoo-Gook would live in this building. The Aleuts were informed that they must go to this Church every Sunday. Anyone who did not go was beaten. However, in spite of the killings and beatings, the Aleuts still prostrated themselves around the Tree stump, and wept, and asked Agoo-Gook to forgive them. Finally, these priests concluded that the Aleuts were too far gone to be saved. They built a little house over the Tree stump that was now in the church yard. Then they took the children into the church and taught them their language. Right now they were telling the children that the little house out in the churchyard with no windows and no doors was filled with evil spirits like the Itty-Gitty. If the children went near this little house the evil spirits would get them just like they had already gotten their mommies and daddies. That is why their mommies and daddies were crying so much because they could not get away from the evil spirits in the little house.

The priests taught the children strange songs, dressed them in robes and had them carry lighted candles. When the Aleuts were forced to go to the Church, the men were made to stand on one side and the women were made to stand on the other. They had to stand for hours and could make no sound. They had no idea what was going on. The place did not have the feeling of peace and love that their Tree had. It was a cold and foreboding place with pictures of a man like them, hanging and bleeding from a cross. Everyone was sure that these priests and men from the ships had done this to that man. They reasoned that the picture was a warning to them that if they did not obey the priests and the men from the ships, they would suffer the same fate.

The young man, his wife and two foster sons reported that they had waited for a dark night to make their escape. They almost drowned getting across Umnak pass, but it would be better to drown in the clean cold sea rather than to be tortured to death slowly on a cross like the man in the picture. Agoo-Gook be praised that they were back with their friends in a snug barabara.

The barabara life style was another thing the strangers did not like, especially because everyone took off all their clothes when they entered. From time to time, they would make surprise raids on the barabaras, and if the people did not have clothes on they would be beaten. These strangers were truly barbarians and uncivilized. They probably realized that their own bodies were ugly and stank and that is why they did not take their clothes off when they came inside.

As more and more refugees and the warriors slowly returned to Unalaska village, Amaknak village, Captains Bay village, and the other villages around Unalaska Bay more horror stories of beatings, killings, rape and slavery were told.

Slowly things, more or less, got back to normal. That winter Kung and Ookig became fathers. Both couples had good sound healthy sons born within a week of each other. The woman, from the pilgrimage, with the two foster sons was now pregnant. She was sure that Agoo-Gook had answered her prayer in spite of the Tree having been cut down. Now she prayed for a baby girl to replace the foster child she had lost.

Then word came that four ships had arrived in Makoshin Bay.   Fear and apprehension ran through the Islands like an ice-cold wind that clothes and heat could not stop. Some of the relatives from Makoshin Village escaped in the winter over Makoshin Pass. These refugees came to another Village up behind the Islands in Captains Bay with frost-bite and frozen children. The ships had taken all their food and supplies. Starvation was rampant. Also many strange diseases began to appear among the people. One called the "coughing sickness" seemed to be caused by being forced to wear clothes in the barabaras. The strangers called it "pneumonia". The other was a red, itchy pimple sickness that the strangers called "measles". Many people in Makoshin were dying from these unheard of sicknesses.

Many Councils were called, and from experience, it was decided to follow the advice given by Ookig, at the Tree, when the strangers had first arrived. They were to be obedient to the strangers and not provoke them. They were to try to learn the secrets of their weapons, try to learn their language in order to understand them better and to be patient. It was also agreed that each family was to build a secret barabara and stash away what-ever food, clothing, tools and weapons they could.

If the men were taken as slaves, the women were to be patient and wait for their men to return. If taken as slaves the men would make every effort to escape and return and take care of their families. The men were also counseled by the slaves, who had already escaped, to be very obedient and not to provoke the ships' crews since this was a sure way to get killed.

The red salmon were just starting to run in the lakes when the stranger's ships sailed into Unalaska bay. They had all the food and water they needed but were short handed. So the strong young men around Unalaska Bay were rounded up from all the villages and taken along with the badarkies aboard the sailing ships. Ookig happened to be up behind the hill in the hidden barabara when the raiding party came through Captains Bay but they took Kung. Ookig heard the commotion and prudently stayed hidden and watched. The women and babies were not molested, so he stayed put.

After the raiding party had gone away with Kung, Ookig returned to their barabara late that night. Annik cried when she saw him, but he went back up to the hidden barabara and stayed there. The raiding sweep was made once more and then the ships sailed out of Unalaska Bay.

There were four ships out in the Bering sea

they headed due north. Kung was put to work putting out and taking in sail. He was quick and nimble in the rigging and learned easily. Some of the Aleut slaves had been captive for over a year and were from places like Adak and even Attu. They could speak Russian and were assigned to teach these newly shanghaied sailors the ropes. The slaves were told that they were going to the Pribilof Islands, where they were to kill and skin fur seal for their captors.

The ships had no rowers and Kung learned that they were driven by the wind. He was always asking questions and listened to the answers very carefully. When he did not understand something he kept at it until he did.

There was a young priest on the same ship with Kung. He was not much older than Kung, and his job was to teach these heathen savages Russian and religion. He was a serious young man and had sailed from mother Russia just that spring. He found in Kung a bright and eager student in both subjects. He was called Father Baranoff. As Kung picked up the language quickly, it was not long before they were able to talk more freely.

Kung was always the first to obey orders. He never argued and soon became a proficient sailor. As his ability in Russian improved, he was moved up to take his watch on the bridge and steer the ship. This gave him further opportunity to polish up his Russian. Everyone on the bridge spoke Russian all the time. When the others were ordered off the ship to club to death the fur seal, and skin them, and then leave all the meat to rot on the Islands, Kung was kept on board.

The fur seal came to the Islands every summer to mate and have their young. They were fairly helpless on land so the hunters would herd them away from the beaches and use a club to kill them and then take the hide. The market for these beautiful pelts fetched a premium price in Moscow.

The young priest told Kung about God and that God had created the world and man and woman. Kung explained that Agoo-Gook was the creator of all that is and he wanted to know the difference, saying it sounded like the Father's God and his Agoo-Gook were the same. The Father then told Kung that his Creator was the real one and Kung's Creator was a false one. Kung didn't argue the point, but in his heart he was sure that it was only a difference of language. The priest wanted to give his star student all the knowledge he had learned in the seminary in Moscow.

The priest one day was explaining about the time of Abraham and the arc of the covenant. How God had told Abraham that this arc and these tablets were a gift from God to man. The covenant was an agreement that God made, and He told Abraham that if he would take care of these tablets, He would be his God and Abraham's people would be His people. Kung then explained that God (he now used the Father's term instead of Agoo-Gook) had also come to his people, the Aleuts, and had made the same covenant, but instead of an arc and tablets he had given his people a Tree where no other trees could grow. He had said, "You take care of this Tree and I will be your God and you will be my people." Kung wanted to know if this was not the same thing, and if it was, why had the Russians cut down the Tree? The Father got angry and said that this was a foolish comparison since what was written was truth and what Kung was saying was superstition. Again Kung said nothing but in his heart he knew if what he said was foolish superstition so was what the Father said, and if what the Father said was truth, then what Kung said was also truth.

The work aboard the ship was heavy and the summer went by quickly. The fur seal had already left the Island. Only two of the ships were loaded and those two would go back to Russia and unload. The other two were to return to Unalaska and winter in Captains Bay up behind the Islands. This was the best place they had found to protect them from the winter storms they knew they would have to face. Fortunately for Kung, his ship had not been loaded.

The priest now told Kung about Jesus, that he brought love to the world. Jesus was God made flesh and everything that He did was filled with love. He told him about how Jesus had saved the woman from being stoned to death:

Jesus, one day came upon a crowd of people gathered around a woman. Jesus asked the people what they were doing. They told Him that this woman had committed adultery and they were going to stone her to death as this was the law. Jesus told the crowd that they must not do that. The people then accused Jesus of changing the law's of Moses. Jesus then told them that if any of them did not have any sin then they could throw the first stone. The crowd dispersed.

Jesus was without sin and could have thrown the stone. He did not. He comforted this terrified woman, and as He wiped away her tears, He told her that God loved her and she was forgiven.

These stories as the Father told them moved

Kung very deeply.

Then Kung asked, "Now let us say that all the Aleuts as you claim are heathens and we had strayed away from the true teachings of God. Let us just suppose that your loving and kind Lord Jesus came to our Island of the Tree on your ship. From what I have learned from you about how loving and kind Jesus was, don't you think He would have come ashore and loved us and through His great love and kindness would have taught us by example how to come to the truth? Do you think your Lord Jesus would come to us with blazing guns and booming cannons, stealing, raping our women, and murdering our people? How is it possible that you come to us in the name of your blessed Savior and commit these heinous crimes in His name? I think He must be weeping in His spiritual home for what you have done and what you are now doing in his name."

The Father had tears in his eyes for in his heart he knew this young man was right. How dare he call himself a Christian and stand by and let these things happen. That evening Father Baranoff transferred to one of the ships going back to Russia and Kung never saw him again.

The ships came into Unalaska bay and dropped anchor in behind the sandspit off of Amaknak. All of the Aleuts were released because the Russians did not want to take care of them through the winter. Kung had been worried sick over his wife and child these past months. He borrowed a badarky from the village on Amaknak and sped off home to Captains Bay village.

-10-

Vasa threw herself into Kung's arms and the baby screamed at this sudden intrusion of a stranger. Between laughter and tears, they shared their experiences. Ookig and Annik had shown their true friendship and saw to it that Vasa and her child wanted for nothing. The hidden warehouse they had stocked up behind the hill had also been a solace for her. The salmon run had been abundant, and several whales had been secured, supplying oil and fresh meat to everyone on Amaknak and Unalaska.

After Kung had told Vasa, Annik and the other friends that gathered that night about his adventures and some of the things he had learned from the Russians, he explained that they must leave the area and flee from these Russians as soon as possible. He explained that while on the ship he had mastered their language and he heard them talk about how many more ships were right now being prepared to sail for their area. The Russians were preparing big fleets to come for the whale, fur seal, sea otters, fish and

148

something they called gold.

Kung further explained that they constantly referred to the Aleuts as an abundant work force. They talked about how there were plenty of able-bodied men they could get from up and down the Aleutian chain. He said he was appalled at the magnitude of their planning and the indiscriminate use of his people as slaves. Kung also explained that he had also found a method of saving themselves. They had a deep-seated fetish about this religion called Christianity. He explained that all the Aleut had to do was say he accepted Jesus Christ as his personal savior, have some water sprinkled on his head and attend their church, and then he or she would no longer be considered a heathen and could not be mistreated. The men called priests on the ships were very powerful.

Kung then said that this Jesus Christ of theirs was the exact same person as their God. He taught the people the same things He had taught the Aleuts, and he had learned this very well from the priest himself. One big difference was that they had killed

Jesus by torturing Him on a cross. The Aleuts had given their God their love, honor and respect. So Kung advised everyone that wished to stay in Unalaska to go to the priest as soon as possible and be saved. If what they tried to teach them was not according to the teachings of God just let it go and try to understand that the priest doing the teaching was wrong not Jesus or Agoo-Gook. It would be like the nonsense they were teaching the children in Nikolski about the little house in the church yard with no windows and no doors. Who really was teaching nonsense and superstition? Kung had discovered nothing in the teachings of Jesus that even came close to this nonsense.

Kung called for a secret meeting of the Chiefs and elders from all the villages from Summers Bay to Ruffs Bay, including all the villages on Amaknak, to advise them of what he had discovered. A few days later the two ships, which had brought Kung home, were seen sailing up behind the islands at the head of Captains Bay.

Kung and Ookig and the other men of Captains Bay village went in their badarkies over to Amaknak village, because it had the largest meeting hall. The place was packed, and Kung told them what he had learned from the Russians. The meeting was held at night so as not to attract the attention of the ship's crews.

It was evening and Vasa and Annik had just finished feeding their babies when one of the ship's whale boats landed on the beach. The men with their guns went through the village and were taking all the young women. They were surprised to find no young men, but pleased because they had come intending to kill them if they resisted the taking of their women. One of the crew made the young woman with the two foster sons stand up, and when he saw that she was heavy with child, he slammed the butt of his gun into her swollen belly. Kung's and Ookig's babies were left on the floor of the barabara screaming, the mothers tried to protest, but they were beaten and dragged off.

The ships' crews had been out to sea for many months and now they wanted some women to keep them company through the winter. They raided all the smaller villages around Captains Bay that evening, including the villages on the south end of Amaknak out near the Rat Islands.

When the men returned from the meeting, they found their barabaras in shambles. The young man's wife had miscarried a dead little girl and was bleeding to death on the floor. She had just enough strength to tell her husband what had happened before she died in his arms. Other details were filled in by the older men and women who had been left behind and the little boys now aged 9 and 11. These old people and children had rescued Ookig's and Kung's babies.

That night a war party was put together of the men in the villages that had lost their wives and daughters. Kung was to lead the war party because he knew every detail of the ships. He explained where the guns and ammunition were kept and where the guards would be if any were on guard. The whole next day was spent in preparation, and it was decided to be a late-night attack after the crews were asleep.

In the late afternoon, Kung went up on the side of Mount Pyramid and prayed to God in the name of Jesus to protect his wife and son. He told God that he really didn't understand why this was happening to him and his people, but was sure in the end God's plan and purpose would be made plain. He also told God that he knew he was helpless in the face of this calamity and could only rely on Him for the safety of his family and himself.

The sky was overcast and a light rain was falling that night so the darkness was complete. The large war party climbed aboard the two ships and they got to the gun magazine and armed themselves. Most of the crew were killed while they slept. A few put up a fight but were killed in the end. The women were released and the ships were sunk. The water was not so deep in behind the islands and so when they sank the ship to the bottom the decks still remained awash on the surface.

The women were hysterical about their children. Some of their men had been killed in the fight. It was over, but now the thought in everyone's mind was to get out of Unalaska Bay as quickly as possible. Kung knew that other ships were coming, but he did not know when. Preparations went forward and some of the families departed for Makoshin and Akutan that very day. The majority of the villages in Unalaska Bay were not overly concerned as they had taken no part in the freeing of the women.

Kung and Ookig were getting their tools, weapons and badarkies ready. Unknown to the Aleuts, however, was that two of the crew of the ill-fated ships had made their escape over Makoshin pass and that three other Russian ships were wintering in Makoshin Bay. These ships had been hunting sea otter and Kung had no knowledge of them. Two ships immediately weighed anchor and headed for Captains Bay. The third went west toward Russia to alert other ships of the full-scale revolt in Unalaska Bay. The two ships arrived and anchored offshore in front of Captains Bay village. All badarkies that were out in the bay were picked up. The escape route was sealed off by these Russian ships. The next day three more ships arrived and they set up patrols across the mouth of Unalaska Bay. The villagers that had left a day earlier were picked up and brought back. The people that had escaped to Makoshin, along with most of the men from there, were also brought to Captains Bay. Ookig, Annik, Vasa and the babies moved out of their barabaras and into the secret warehouse behind the hill.

The men from all over Unalaska Island were being rounded up and brought to Captains Bay. Ookig who had gone to the river for water was captured and tied up with the other men. They even took the man and his two little boys. It was evident that they were taking little boys as young as six or seven years old. Old age was no barrier either. They took the aged people as well. On the third day they lined up the men whose hands were tied and then made bets with each other as to how many men one bullet could kill. The mass genocide of the Aleut people was underway.

Kung crawled up to the top of the hill, and Annik took her baby and went to her husband. When

Annik came Ookig screamed at her to go back. One of the guards motioned her away, and when she refused to go, he smashed in her face with the butt of his gun. The baby fell to the ground with his mother and started to scream. The guard smashed in the baby's head in the same way. Ookig who was very strong, broke free and was able to break the guards neck before he was shot down.

Kung felt sick and could watch no more. The shootings went on day and night and because they were so close to the village they did not dare try to escape. The next morning after the killings had begun Kung was again on the hill hidden in the tall grass.

An Aleut man, who had been a slave on a Russian ship for sometime and had even been to Russia and was brought all the way from Kashiga and could not in any way possible been in the party that freed the women from the would-be rapers, he declared to the Russian Captain in perfect Russian that he was a Christian, had been baptized and had no part in the war party that raided the Russian ships. The Russian captain told him that killing innocent

Russian sailors was not the act of a Christian. The man replied that stealing and raping other men's wives was not the act of a Christian either. The Captain turned red in the face and ran his sword through the tied man.

The dead bodies were strewn from the cliffs before Pyramid Creek to the cliffs south of the village at Captains Bay.

-12-

That night it was pitch black due to a heavy overcast, and Kung, Vasa and the baby, with packs on their backs and remembering the stories of the Biorka Pass, slipped out of their hidden warehouse and went up behind Pyramid Mountain and into Biorka Pass and over to Beaver Inlet. There were no Russian boats in Beaver Inlet. At the village at the end of the pass on the inlet side they were given a badarky, tools and weapons. Also Kung had the gun and ammunition he had taken from the Russian ship when he went to rescue his wife.

He shared with the villagers the wholesale slaughter at the Tree and what had just taken place at Captains Bay in Unalaska Harbor. The people here had not seen any Russians yet, and Kung tried his best to give them as much advice as he could. At each village they stopped, he showed the gun and advised the people of the blood-thirsty Russians that were looting, killing and raping wherever they appeared.

They had the same weather problems going back toward Kodiak as they had going to the Holy Tree. The addition of the out-riggers was a big help in stabilizing their tiny craft. In Sandpoint, where they stopped for several weeks, Kung and Vasa tanned some hides and sewed them together and Kung rigged them up as a sail on a two-hole badarky. This was a wonderful invention that Kung had learned to manage from the Russians. This relieved them from a great deal of rowing, so in this land called "The Birthplace of The Winds" they never lacked for a power source.

It was mid winter when Kung and Vasa presented their son to her parents in Chignik where they settled down. When the Russian ships finally made their appearance in Chignik the people were ready and had already started to build a church after the style of the one built in Unalaska village. The Russians were met by a strong Christian man who spoke fluent Russian and when questioned by the priests, Kung knew all the answers. The priests renamed him at his baptism, Christianson, or son of Christ. His descendants to this day are found up and down the Aleutian chain. One thing the Russians never found out about this son of Christ was that most of the answers he gave them were from his knowledge of Agoo-Gook.